DOMINOES and CUPS

novel inspired by true events

DAISY HARRIETTE T. A. HEISLER

ISBN: 978-1-7772960-0-1 Printed Book
ISBN: 978-1-7772960-1-8 Electronic Book

Where the story may resemble a person, names have been
changed to protect the privacy of individuals.

Email author through website:
http://www.DaisyHarrietteHeisler.com

Table of contents

Dedicated to all the dogs, cats and horses
who have been faithful and unconditional loves of my life
and will never read this book
and
to all the people who have not walked in my footsteps
but are curious

chapter one

Dominoes

Dominoes—life is like a set of dominoes. It is a game of matching and building. In life, one event follows another. Each event is a result of the one that came before. If the domino blocks are set up in rows, when one falls so does the whole line because each block is affected by the block behind and affects what is to come. If domino blocks build a tower or wall, they are supported by what came before but are not permanent—the blocks freely fall to their original state, ready to be built again. Such is life. Such is birth choices, life lived and followed by death. Such is the original soul and the energy between the movement of domino blocks.

Spirit speaks:
"Who am I? I have the assignment to be Mary's spirit guardian. Mary will need me to help her in the events of her life as it unfolds and with choices she will make. I am invisible energy surrounding her life. I know a larger picture than the

confinements of life as it is lived day by day in earthly time. She
will learn in this lifetime.

"The knowledge of me will come to her in time. Right now she
is unaware of me — but she has questions about life that stir from
her unconscious self. Like bubbles, the questions form, float briefly
on waves of air, burst and disappear in daily activity of her
childish life, only to be formed again.

"Mary does not realize just yet that she was born with
extrasensory perception. She is thinking her way of understanding
life is how everyone feels and sees life. She does not yet realize that
this perception may be perceived by others as silly and wrong.
Mary will have to be strong within herself."

Mary was almost two years old and had just mastered the
ability to talk in full sentences. Every evening, she and her
father laid in bed beside each other as he read the comics
from the daily newspaper to her. She always had one leg
under the blankets and one leg on top of the blankets as she
listened to his velvety voice and followed his finger
pointing out the pictures for her to follow the story. One
evening, she was aware of a man standing in the bedroom
by the armoire. He wore a long coat and a large hat. He
would stand there and look intently at Mary with deep,
brown colored eyes.

The man appeared every evening to look intently at
Mary as her father read the comics to her, and every time,
she would pull her bare leg from outside the covers to
covering her leg. The look that seemed to penetrate deep
into Mary, unsettled her.

She told her parents about the man. They moved out of the house because he was not a living being. He was a ghost.

He did not follow to their new home.

It was Christmas when a gift of dominoes was placed in five year old Mary's hands. Mary's father had made the domino blocks for her. He had just bought a house for the family, so he crafted gifts for the children this year.

She unwrapped the game amidst cheers and laughter of her brothers and sisters opening their own gifts.

Mary opened the box and looked at the little black blocks with white dots and wondered what they were all about. As usual, her father noticed. He knelt down on the floor and started to stand the blocks upright in a long row. Mary got the idea and helped.

"Now, Mary," he said, "put your finger against the block at this end of the line and give it a little push."

She was fascinated as the blocks fell one by one until the last block fell.

Wood was burning in the kitchen stove to keep the room warm. It was evening bath time in the kitchen. A small tub of warm water was set up on the table and towels were spread out over the table. One by one, the smaller babies and toddlers were sponge bathed by their mother. The sounds in the room were soothing as each child was bathed, towelled and small feet pounded the floor as naked bodies ran off.

It was Mary's turn. She was the oldest and last to be bathed. She sat naked on the table as her mother started to sponge her with warm suds. She always marvelled at the gentleness of her mother. Her mother sponged her belly and hesitated as she commented, "You have the brown line on your stomach that only women who have given birth to a baby have. How strange!"

Then, as usual, her mother pointed out the birth mark on Mary's ankle. "My mother had the exact same birthmark you have."

Mary had heard it before and wondered what it all meant.

Over her young years, because Mary was the oldest child, her mother often talked to her about her own mother, usually as she ironed clothing; Mary would sit nearby, watching and listening. If cooking, Mary would stand beside her mother and together they would roll dough in their hands and drop the noodles into boiling water as her mother would describe her own childhood. At a young age, Mary understood that her mother was still young and close to her own childhood, and that she needed to talk about it. She grew to feel protective of her mother and listened with compassion.

She knew that her mother's mother had died after giving birth to a baby girl when her mother was only six years old. She understood that her mother's mother was her grandmother. It seemed so sad to Mary that her grandmother died and left small children behind.

She heard about the family tree. Mary knew that her grandmother had been an immigrant in her early twenties and had traveled to Canada by boat. She had lived common-law with Mary's grandfather because his wife in Europe refused to immigrate with him and would not divorce. Even though he had been owner of a hotel with a vineyard, he was also a soldier on horseback and ordered by the Russians to harm the Ukrainian people. A bounty was placed on his head by the Russians for helping the Ukrainian people instead of carrying out orders to harm them. He left everything behind, escaping into Germany and from there he immigrated to Canada. His brother was not so lucky—he was captured and sent to Siberia to do hard labor and was never heard from again.

In her mother's stories, Mary soon understood that common-law was frowned upon by society in Canada, so it was a secret that her grandparents were not officially married.

The 1918 flu pandemic spread around the world and into 1920. In 1920, their infant son died of the flu. Mary's mother often described how as small child, she stood beside her mother as she washed her baby boy laying dead on the table. Even as a child, Mary always felt the pain of this story.

Mary's grandmother had given birth to all her children at home, which was usual for the early 1900s. For the birth of her fifth child very soon after the death of her son, her husband gave her an expensive special gift of being able to give birth in a hospital where she would have all the special care and rest that he thought she should have.

She never went home. On the third day after giving birth to a girl, she died of a hospital borne infection. Mary grew up with the knowledge that her grandmother died in childbirth. She also grew up thinking that if her grandmother had stayed home for the birth, she might still be alive. This thought would be important in decisions later in Mary's life.

Mary felt the sorrow of her grandmother leaving behind three small children, a newborn baby and a grieving husband who would have to take care of the children and work to support them at the same time.

The dilemma was partially solved by a relative that her grandfather had sponsored to immigrate to Canada, taking the newborn and the next youngest child into her care in her own home. That left Mary's mother and her brother in the care of her father.

Mary's mother was horrified when she watched the woman caring for her newborn baby sister put the baby bottles on the windowsill and flies would sit on the nipples. Then the woman would pick up the bottles and put the nipples into the baby's mouth. The baby died suddenly.

Mary's mother lived with the knowledge of why her baby sister died and held blame which caused her never to like the woman later. It weighed on her that she had not been able to help her baby sister. She compensated by being the best daughter she could be. She taught herself how to cook and clean house. She would run home from school to cook meals for her father so that he could come home after a long hard day at work to a wholesome meal that always had a soup along with a hearty main course.

Mary had moments of wondering if she was her own grandmother. It was a strange thought that came and went. No one talked about reincarnation around Mary, so the notion came from Mary herself. Her mother never hinted at it even though she pointed out the brown line on Mary's belly and the birthmark. Mary had a life to live, so all this knowledge and wondering about her grandmother was only background commotion to her sense of joy in each new day.

Mary's favorite uncle John, her mother's brother was a soldier in the World War II. At age seven, while watching a news clip of the second world war. Mary had a foreknowledge that seemed like a dagger into her body. The premonition was that she would marry a boy who had lived in that war. Again, she could not shake the idea away. It did not feel exciting. It felt more like a deed to do and kind of sad.

Life was full of sunshine and fun. Mary ran barefoot in summer through endless dandelion fields and sat in a path of the garden to eat whatever was growing. She would watch the life cycle of the caterpillars turning into butterflies and wonder about life for everyone. She would contemplate what her own life cycle might be. She wondered about heaven and hell and what is the difference between a caterpillar and herself.

In winter when ice and snow covered the ground, and the air was so cold that it made every breath ice crystals in the air, she would examine the sky. In all the cold, the sky seemed to be more illuminated than any other time of the year. Looking at the millions of stars and the space between, she wondered about life. Over and over, she asked the same questions about who she was and why was she born on earth. But, life was full of fun — skating on the rink and her father showing off to the young boys as he jumped a snowbank on skates — or in summer, her father diving off a high diving board to land in a bellyflop — Mary swimming the whole summer away — and having cats and dogs as pets

—riding horses on the farm. It was all too much fun to worry about whether or not she was her own grandmother.

Mary grew up knowing that her father was a water diviner and had found clean water for farmers. To her, it was a completely natural thing to do. He took her along with her brothers and sisters out to the prairie farming fields and taught them to be water diviners. They watched as he picked out willow branches and whittled them with his pocket knife into the forked shape he liked and gave a branch to each of his children. He taught them how to hold the branch in two hands as they walked slowly across the fields.

Mary would hold her willow branch and marvel that it would dip and tug alongside his branch. Her hands and arms could feel the strength of an unseen force working the twig. Her father would explain the meaning of how deep and what color the water was that ran underground, and which direction it flowed.

She was filled with awe that the willow twigs could tell so much about what was so deep below the ground where they walked. But, more than that, her father knew how to understand the information given to him. His successes proved that when the wells were dug.

Her father was delighted, telling her, "You have the gift! You should never use gifts selfishly. Never take money for gifts of this kind. The gift has been given to you and you must use it to be helpful to others."

Her father had set her up to look at life, healing, talents and successes based on energy as a gift not to be used selfishly.

Mary was twelve years old when she sat in a circle with three girlfriends. The girls had heard that if you hold a needle on a thread over the palm of the hand and ask a question, the needle would turn in circles left or right and answer the question.

The question burning on the minds of the girls was about future husbands. They wanted to know how many times they would marry. The needle answered each girl with one or two marriages, causing each girl to be satisfied. Mary's turn was last. She asked the question. The needle told her that she would have four husbands. The other girls laughed. Mary was upset over her answer because all she wanted was one husband.

It had been a great joke to play with the needle and thread, but over the next few days Mary could not shake off the foretelling of four marriages. The question of what energy caused the needle to spin bothered Mary.

Mary's mother had always told her to marry only for love and that money was not important if you have love. That is what Mary was determined to do; she would marry for love only once for the rest of her life.

She thought — *the heck with what a stupid needle and thread said in a game.*

She got on with her life. She followed girlfriends to ball games, hockey game, concerts in the park where her friends were hoping to meets guys. Mary was just a tag along having fun.

At age fourteen, she and a girlfriend would sneak away on Sundays. They would take a Greyhound bus on their weekly allowances and go to a horse farm that rented horses to ride by the hour. That's where she met a guy known as Cisco Kid. At first glance, he was dressed in a black western outfit like the Cisco Kid of the movies. When he introduced himself, his accent gave him away. He was a recent immigrant from Germany and fascinated with the western way of life.

Cisco Kid was hungry and broke, so Mary walked into the nearby town and bought fish and chips to give to him. That did it! He was interested in Mary.

Mary was interested. He was handsome with black hair slicked back and deep blue eyes that were like looking into pools of deep clear water. He looked different than all the boys she had every met. Her romantic fantasies emerged.

Back in the city, she would discover that when not wearing his Cisco Kid costume, he was an immaculate dresser. A tailor by trade, his suits were all hand made. His shirts were clean all the time and pressed in his very special way.

He also had other romantic interests. One of his girlfriends sat in front of Mary in a high school class. Mary would look at the girl's back—her slender body and short, neat black hair and feel plain in comparison. But over time, Cisco Kid was spending more and more time with Mary and her family. Soon there were no other girlfriends. Mary was the only one. He tried to move in with the family but was turned down by Mary's parents. Determined to be close, he moved into a basement suite in the house right next door—the house where Mary's piano teacher lived.

Cisco's war experience was still with him. He spent hours with a paper and pencil, drawing war scenes with planes overhead shooting at each other. It was fascinating to Mary's brothers.

Cisco and Mary went to ballroom dances that her parents had always gone to. Mary's father had taught her how to do the waltzes, polkas, and two steps, but now she was doing new dances with Cisco. He taught her how to dance the tango, the rumba, and cha cha making her feel more worldly. She had jived with girlfriends in their living rooms, but now she jived up a storm with Cisco in a ballroom. She was flying in all directions over Cisco's shoulders and under his legs. It was a ball, doing all the dances that she had not done before.

Cisco was a singer, coming from grandparents who were a concert soprano and a violinist. Cisco would get up on stage at every dance and do a segment of songs. He was attractive to many women who awed and swooned over him. One woman was so enthralled by Cisco that she proposed to her husband that he bring Cisco to her so that she could have sex with him right in their bed. The husband did so, but unfortunately for his wife, Cisco had brought Mary along and did not comply with her wish. It was only when they arrived at the house that Mary found out what the request had been. It was a sex education that a young girl had not even imagined.

Cisco explained to Mary that his sex eduction had been by an older woman who taught him every thing he knew. It boggled Mary's way of thinking, but he explained that was a way of life where he grew up.

Mary's world had expanded, which is what she had craved all her life. She had gained knowledge of more than prairie life—some of it shocking and some of enjoyable. Then four years later, Mary had lost interest in Cisco as a possible husband. After being expelled from school more than once for playing hooky, she was now a working girl in her first job and all her income was being eaten up by her boyfriend for his gambling and drinking. She was always broke. More than that, she was not in love. Her fantasy had ended.

At Mary's place of work, she discovered other men were interested in her and she was interested in exploring. She wanted to end the relationship without hurting Cisco. She thought that if she proposed marriage, he would refuse to get married. Then she would have her freedom back.

One evening, as they sat in his old car in a field by the railway track, she proposed marriage.

He got excited. "Yes! Let's get married right away."

Mary was shocked. Her plan had failed. She felt trapped.

chapter two

Husband One

S pirit speaks:
"*Until now, Mary has been enjoying life as a young person with no concerns except for a desire to protect her parents from life's disappointments. On the other hand, she knows that she has caused her parents to worry because of her zest to run free, like the day she came out of the hospital after having her tonsils removed. Her parents tried to protect her by keeping her indoors for just one day, but she ran out when they were not looking and joined the kids in the empty lot across the street as they played games that included a lot of running around.*

"She has always thought of her mother as too good a soul for this world. She would watch her mother in the garden making friends with insects and wonder about such a beautiful soul. Mary was thinking of herself as less than that beautiful or good.

"She has disappointed her mother in several ways. Her mother read an article in the newspaper to her because the girl who lived down the street took first prize in a major piano recital. Her mother's sadness that Mary had not achieved that acclaim, caused her to quit piano lessons. In elementary school, she had

often arrived late because she looked at the world upside down too long on the stunt pole in the playground on the way to school. Her mother cried when Mary played hooky from high school and got expelled twice.

"Mary would watch the girls in the church choir who seemed perfectly angelic and wonder how she could ever be that way. Then, she would go about her merry way and not worry about being angelic. Life was just too much fun to be prefect and not get into trouble.

"Up to now, Mary has been protected by her parents. Her father from farming roots has been hard working and has kept the home warm, and has been the provider of real, healthy food to nourish his family. He was Mary's example of a good man with a zest for life like she had. Her mother cooked healthy meals daily and cared for her family with gentleness. She did her best to teach Mary what she knew.

"Mary discovered that in the evenings when her mother had finished her day's work, she would read magazine articles that included other trains of thought, other cultures, other beliefs in life and death that were not just angels and heaven.

"Mary's uncles and aunts along with her parents at her grandparents' farm after a big supper, would sit on the floor around the walls of the living room by lantern light, telling stories about strange energies. One story Mary was particularly fond of was the story about the money fire — the story was told that Mary's father and some brothers built a bonfire that they sat around while talking one evening and when the fire was put out, a bunch of coins were in the ashes. Stories like this were normal to Mary.

"Following her childhood, Mary is approaching another domino. Her premonition of marrying a child of war will now

become reality. She will now face a battle like she has no knowledge of how to handle."

Mary nervously entered the kitchen to talk to her parents. Her father was sitting by the kitchen table. Her mother was cooking something at the kitchen stove. Mary stood in the middle of the kitchen facing her father.

"I'm going to marry Cisco."

Her father looked distressed, said nothing for a long minute and then he quietly gave advice, "You should wait."

"Why?

"I don't think he is ready for marriage."

"I've already said I will marry him."

"Wait. My father died less than a month ago. It is not the time to have a wedding. Wait."

Mary paused in sympathy. "Dad, he has already set the date for February — next month."

Her father was getting angry. "You can't have my permission! It's not the time! Wait!"

Then her stubbornness took over. "I don't need your permission. I'm eighteen...old enough to make my own decisions."

"If you insist, I will not attend your wedding and I won't allow family to attend. I'm asking you to wait."

Mary glanced at her mother. Her mother's face said it all. It was white with pain. She was not an argumentative person so she remained silent.

Mary turned and went up the stairs to her bedroom. She sat on her bed feeling sad and torn. She had made a promise and her father was asking her to break it. Who would she disappoint?

Mary entered a dress shop.

"I am getting married. I need a wedding dress."

The saleswoman walked across the room to a white dress hanging among all the other day dresses. She pulled out the only wedding dress in the whole shop. It was formal with a lace overlay, strapless with a matching bolero—everything Mary thought a wedding dress should look like and it was Mary's size. She tried it on. It fit perfectly.

The saleswoman brought out a headdress crusted with shiny stones. It was all perfect. More than that, it all cost the exact amount of money Mary had in her purse. Mary thought the whole experience was surreal because—*how on earth could there have been only one dress in my exact size and exact money?* It seemed as though it was waiting for her.

She took the bag with her wedding costume home and snuck it into the house. Her mother's face haunted her as she hid the bag under her bed.

For the next few days, she slept over the dress and wondered—*why am I getting married to a man I do not love?*—*why am I not getting out of the stupid situation of a bad idea to propose marriage?* She knew why. It had been a rape one evening in a park, but she did not see it that way.

She was only fourteen years old and did not recognize rape. Instead, she blamed herself for being in the situation where it happened. She had willingly gotten into a car with Cisco and two other men. When they drove to the park and parked the car in a secluded area among the trees and bushes, the two other men got out of the car and walked away. Mary was innocent of recognizing what was happening. All she knew was that she was alone with Cisco in the dark of the night hidden somewhere in the bushes and thought nothing of it until he started to explain what happens in sex. Mary had no idea except what she had read in a pocketbook story with her friends and it was not explicit—just enough to entice young girls to read the book and feel they got a sex education.

The men who had walked away returned after a convenient length of time. Mary was highly embarrassed, knowing they were complicit with whatever happened and she was in physical pain that only she would know about.

She thought she needed to marry Cisco because she was no longer a virgin and needed to marry the man who took it for himself.

The wedding day arrived. Her father had not relented. Mary understood that no family member was going to be allowed to attend her wedding.

It was an icy February morning. Somehow, wedding plans had been made. Mary had no idea who made them. All she knew was that she had not been invited to be a part of the arrangements for her own wedding and she really did not care. Her only responsibilities were to get the wedding cake to the reception room in the German restaurant in the morning and to be present at the wedding in the afternoon and to attend the reception following.

She left the house early to catch a bus to the bakery where her cake had been made.

Arriving at the bakery, she paid for the cake that was wrapped carefully for delivery. Lifting it was a problem. It was a three tier fruit cake, high and heavy. She carried it to the bus stop and caught another bus. Sitting on the bus with the weight of the cake on her lap, she wondered — *why am I doing any of this?* It all seemed unreal.

At the restaurant, she was treated with disdain by the female owner who was preparing the room for the wedding reception. Mary did not feel like introducing herself to such a rude person. She simply handed over the cake, allowing the woman to think she was just the delivery person.

Back home in her bedroom, Mary pulled the bag out from under her bed. She opened it and stared at the white lace. It was all about to happen. This dress would change her life. She would be leaving the security of her parents' home. For the past week, she had eaten more than she usually eats of her mother's suppers because she was afraid she would never eat her mother's cooking again. Instead of looking forward to be married, she was feeling sad at the thought of leaving home.

Slowly, she put the dress on and combed her hair. The tiara across the top of her head picked up light and framed her face with dancing sparkles. She stood in front of the dresser mirror and stared. This was the same dresser mirror in which she had watched herself grow up. She had watched herself as a child, then a little older and putting on her first bra — wearing the mauve formal gown her mother had sewn for her so that she could sing on stage with a group of school children because she had been chosen — then as a girl getting ready to go to a dance with her first and only boyfriend — wearing her mother's green taffeta dancing dress without asking and sneaking out to a dance in it and then coming home with the dress torn under both sleeves because she had been jiving wildly with her boyfriend — always seeing herself just right as a healthy, free girl with just the right body and face to get into a lot of mischief. Now the woman in the mirror looking back at her had finally achieved an angelic look in her white wedding dress and tiara, and she was after all a beautiful woman. But, she was sad.

She made her way down the stairs. Her family was in the living room watching the Saturday shows on television.

She walked into the living room. Her parents looked up in shock.

No one said anything.

Mary turned on her heels and ran toward the door. On the way, she grabbed her coat and flung it over her shoulders. She ran out into the ice and snow.

The church chapel was empty except for the minister and the man and wife duo that Cisco had asked to be best man and maid of honour. Mary had not asked anyone because if her family was not there, she really did not care who witnessed the wedding.

The minister was reading what-ever. Mary was not hearing what he was saying. All she was thinking and feeling was that she was marrying with no love for the man and it was all a mistake. As she stood in her white wedding dress beside her groom, tears filled her eyes and rolled down her cheeks. She wondered if the minister thought she was crying with happiness.

Walking into the restaurant reception room in her wedding dress, the woman who had been so rude in the morning, was visibly shocked and embarrassed as she recognized

Mary now in her wedding dress. Neither said anything. Cisco's German friends filled the room. There was food and gifts. Mary swallowed an oyster for the first time in her life. She thought that was the highlight of the reception.

Regardless of her father's refusal to allow family to attend, Mary's brother showed up.

He took Mary aside to tell her what he had overheard. "Cisco's friends are telling him that if you don't behave as a wife, he should beat you."

Mary realized that not only was she not in love, but she was possibly in danger, and furthermore, his friends were not her friends. She knew Cisco would follow the advice of his men friends.

Over the next weeks, Cisco reminded Mary often, "I want a son to carry on my family name."

It was a couple of months after the wedding when Mary was awfully sick. Thinking she must be dying, she went to see a doctor.

"Good news," he announced. "You are not dying, you are pregnant."

She was surprised. She wandered out of the doctor's office and into a five and dime store to look at baby clothes. She had no money to buy anything, but she could look and make the news come to reality. She fondled a few tiny shirts and pyjamas. At least she could feel the softness and imagine her baby in these clothes.

Even though she had a job, she was always with no money because her husband drank, partied and gambled all the money away. It had been her responsibility to keep paying the rent and buy food.

She had changed jobs after her wedding and at the first interview for the new job in the Workman's Compensation Administration, she had been asked if she was pregnant. She felt invaded by the male interviewer, but she answer honestly, "No," and was hired.

When Mary found out she was pregnant, she confided in the woman who worked at the neighboring desk. Her co-worker reported Mary for being pregnant. Mary got fired.

Finding a new job when she was so sick all day and night—not just in the morning, was not possible. Now she would have to rely on whatever income her husband had left over for the household.

Four months pregnant was when Mary saw the brown line running from her belly button downward. She was reminded of the brown line her mother had pointed out when she was a small child sitting on the table for her bath. That early brown line had disappeared somewhere, sometime, long ago and she had forgotten about it. Now she wondered about it again and wondered how she could have had this line of pregnancy in early childhood. It somehow brought back vivid thoughts about her grandmother who died in childbirth. Mary's secret question about whether or not she was her own grandmother arose again. The thought came and went.

She was alone most of the time. When Cisco was not working, he was out somewhere. She never knew where. She sat in bed in the evenings eating chocolate cake and oranges. She had a craving for sour cabbage rolls over mashed potatoes at the German restaurant and Chinese food. Whenever she had enough money she would wait by herself outside on the front steps in the middle of the night for a delivery of Chinese food.

Her husband came home in the middle of one of those nights with grass stains on the knees of his pants. Mary asked how that happened.

"I was playing chicken in a farm field," was his answer.

She knew he was lying and did not care to know more.

It was the New Year's Eve when she was nine months pregnant that was the most telling. She was alone all evening, not knowing where her husband was. He had gone out to party with his friends and she had not been invited along. At a few minutes after midnight, he came into the house with another guy and two young women. They joyfully wished her a happy new year and all four went out again, leaving her alone. The silence was deafening. Mary wondered how the women, who could see that she was pregnant, just wandered in an out of her house so easily and joyfully.

When Mary was in early labor, she went to her parents' home to wait until it was time to go to the hospital. Her father had to go to work because he was on night shift. She had to take a cab by herself to the hospital.

In front of the hospital doors, she got out of the cab and walked up the steps. The big brown double doors were locked. She wrung the bell. A nun opened the door and said, "We're closed for the night."

Mary pleaded, "I'm in labor. My doctor expects me to be here at this hospital."

The nun shut the door in Mary's face.

Mary was stunned. She wondered what she would do now in the middle of a cold winter evening. Turning around, she realized the cab driver had not gone away. He was waiting for her.

He called to her. "Come. I will take you to the other hospital."

When she got into the cab, he explained. "I've seen it before. Don't worry, I won't charge you for the trip to the other hospital."

What just happened was that this man was acting like her father to protect her. She was in labor and hardly able to speak, but she tried to tell him how grateful she was.

After hours that turned into three days of labor, Mary was wheeled into a delivery room. Without a word, nurses immediately grabbed her arms and shackled her wrists to the flat gurney. Her legs were spread wide apart and shackled at the ankles so that she could not move any part of her body. The room quickly filled with a dozen strangers, mostly men, who were onlookers lining all the walls.

Mary panicked and started to complain about all the onlookers. "I don't want all those men watching. No one told me …"

She was shut up with a cup of ether slapped over her mouth and nose. The window at the side of the room spun around overhead and she was gone.

She woke up in a bed. She looked around and saw the woman in the next bed was the same woman who had her fired from her job. The woman had also given birth and now they were to spend the next few days side by side again.

Mary had a new baby to meet and was not going to concern herself with the woman next door.

Her doctor appeared. He explained that he had to use forceps to deliver her baby because the baby was sideways. He hoped there was no damage other than a few bruises. Then Mary lay there worrying until she could see her baby. Four hour intervals was the only way any mother could see her baby, no matter what else might be of concern.

Mary was still a teenager, just turned nineteen. She was not used to these kinds of troubles and rather than start arguments over what had just happened in the delivery room, she was silent about everything. But, she felt violated and knew her baby had also been violated.

The joy of holding her baby helped to heal it all. As far as she could tell, he was fine — except for the black and blue bruises.

A week later, she went home by cab, again all by herself. Entering her home was a shock. Beer bottles were thrown everywhere. The house looked like it had been turned upside down. The floor in every room was covered in mud with spilled beer puddles everywhere.

There was not a drop of water in the house and no food. Because the house did not have running water, Mary had to leave her baby wrapped in his blanket and take the pail to the corner of a street across the icy road to pump water and carry a heavy pail of water back to the house.

Mary realized that no woman should ever come home with a new baby to this kind of a mess. She had no choice but to deal with it and clean up.

Her husband arrived home. "There's no bread in the house," he complained. That was his greeting.

She asked him why the house was so dirty.

He answered, "We had a party celebrating my son being born. We measured our penises."

"With my tape measure? Or my ruler?"

He did not answer.

She was disgusted. Instead of arguing, she cleaned the house.

Two weeks after the birth of her baby, Mary dressed in her slim fitting red dress with silver threads running through it. She marvelled that her figure looked like it did before she got pregnant. She thought she would look pretty good to Cisco and his friends.

It was a Saturday night and they were going to the dance in the city ballroom as they had done many Saturday's while they were still single.

Mary's parents were usually dancing there Saturday evenings, but they preferred to stay home and babysit their grandchild so that Mary could go out.

The ballroom was crowded. After a couple of dances with her husband, Mary sat at a table with Cisco's friends at the edge of the dance floor. He had disappeared.

Mary's eyes casually wandered upward to the balcony above her. She was shocked to see Cisco kissing a woman with short dark hair, someone Mary did not know.

She slipped away from the table and walked quickly up the stairs. At the top of the stairs, she saw that Cisco and the woman were still embraced and kissing. She walked up to them and stood beside them until they noticed her.

Cisco and the woman looked at her in surprise and said nothing.

Mary had nothing to say to Cisco, but to the woman, she said, "You've got a black moustache."

Cisco was in the habit of blackening his moustache and now she was wearing it. The woman ran to the nearest washroom. As disgusted as Mary was, her sense of comedy got to her. She thought it hilarious even though outwardly she did not show it. Embarrassed, Cisco stood beside her not knowing what to do as he watched the woman run away.

Mary was angry afterward, thinking that she had shown up to the dance in perfect physical shape after having a baby and her husband was not appreciative at all.

The day came when she told Cisco she wanted to leave with her baby. Cisco grabbed his shotgun from the wall and pointed it at her.

"If you try to leave, I'll shoot you."

Looking down the barrel of the gun with a crazed, red faced Cisco angrily at the other end, her mind did a tumble. She had a baby to protect. She believed he would kill her, if not on purpose, maybe by accident in a rage. She would bide her time.

She decided to try and get help. It seemed to her that the minister who married them should be the person to help. The minister sat patiently in his black suit and listened to her story. Then, he said, "I would have beaten you myself. You are married. You cannot leave."

"But he acts like he is not married and he pointed a gun at me."

"Go home."

Mary went home feeling horrified that a minister of the church would insist she stay in such a marriage. Not only that, a minister of the church said he would have beaten her.

She tried to find other help, but there was none.

She needed to find a job and a babysitter. A girlfriend she had chummed with in her teenage years, actually one of the girls who had done the needle and thread with her, offered to babysit because she was a stay at home mom with her toddler.

Mary took a job in a lawyer's office but found it difficult to concentrate. Her mind was on her baby who was still tiny.

On a hot day after work, she made her way to the babysitter's house. Her baby was lying in his wool sweater and bonnet and still in the same diaper that he was wearing when she dropped him off in the morning. The only thing that changed in all the hours was that he was covered with bruises. He had been neglected and beaten at the same time.

It was a long, hot bus ride home. Mary was in desperate need of help. She had an injured baby who had suffered all day long while she was at work. She now had no babysitter and a job she did not feel right in. She had a husband who was absolutely no help and was a big problem.

She was too ashamed to tell her parents about what a mess she had made of her life, so she kept it all a secret from them. The worse it got, the more she did not want to share her troubles and admit such failure. She felt that she had no one to talk with.

Over night, Mary found a new babysitter. This time, it was the mother of a boy she had gone to school with. Mary felt confident that the woman would take good care of her baby.

Back at work, two young lawyers gave her assignments to be completed immediately. They were competing for her time. It was up to her to do one or the other and whichever one did not get done, would be a problem. She completed the day and refused to show up for work the next day. Her thoughts were — *let them do it themselves. I'm not choosing one. I'll not do either one.* She spent the day with her baby instead.

She arrived back at work the following day and was fired.

Life at home was getting violent. Drunken rages were more frequent. Now it was Mary who had the bruises and was afraid her baby would be the victim of his rages one day.

After a beating, she had called the police. They told her they could not interfere in domestic affairs, but she could press charges. Her only choice was to go to court and maybe send Cisco to jail. He would have a criminal record in his new country. She could not do that to him. Her sympathy for him took over. She realized that having sympathy for the man who treated her so badly was stupid. She rationalized not doing anything to hurt him.

Mary's sympathy was based on what she knew about the child who had lived in the midst of the war in Germany. His father had been a soldier fighting for Germany and was killed in Italy. Cisco was the oldest son and felt a responsibility for his mother and brothers. One day, he and his brother were playing in the street — his brother picked up a live grenade and was blown up right in front of Cisco's eyes. He lived with the guilt that his brother lost his life while in his care. He blamed himself. He watched his baby brother die of starvation while his family was running away from the Russians. They were running from East German to West Germany. He and his mother buried the baby in a graveyard enroute and left the baby carriage on the grave. Following that, at a railway station they met a woman in labor. Cisco's mother was helping her with the birth behind a bush when they were approached by a band of men from the far East. The men raped both women. The woman giving birth died along with her baby right there by the train station. His mother was traumatized. Cisco and his two living brothers were traumatized.

As a young teenaged boy, Cisco was helpless in all situations. Then he was taken into the Hitler Youth and brainwashed. His way of thinking was to be forever changed. After that, he was angry at his mother because she made friends with American soldiers to get food for the family.

He left Germany to immigrate and start a new life as soon as he could.

Mary needed to find another job while covered with bruises. She was hired by a political party leader. It was just the two of them working the office. She was only in the job a few days when he grabbed her and hugged her with intentions of more.

It was obvious to Mary that he had seen her as vulnerable. Insulted, she walked out of the office and never bothered to collect her pay check.

Cisco joined the army suddenly without telling Mary and took off by train without a goodbye. Instead, he had partied with his friends until train time. She did not know if she would ever see Cisco again.

Mary believed she was now a single parent with a baby just learning to walk, but more than that, she was pregnant.

She was working for a fruit and vegetable wholesaler. Regardless of feeling nauseated because of the pregnancy, in the mornings she and her baby would walk along the streets on the way to the babysitter and stop to pet the horses pulling delivery carts of milk. Getting to work on time was always a problem, but the slow walks were a time of tranquility with her baby that would be a memory in her mind for the rest of her life.

Her supervisor in the office was a woman with short, brown, greasy hair and big bones that rivalled most men for size. She offered Mary a ride home one hot day. Mary accepted.

Without explaining, the woman drove the opposite way of Mary's home. She took a route through the secluded area of the forested park by the lake where Mary had been raped as a young girl.

Mary was scared that once again she was in a situation that she did not know how to get out of, except to jump out of a moving car. After an initial complaint that she wanted to go straight home and there was no response from the woman who was looking straight ahead, Mary silently prayed intensely for protection.

To her surprise, the car did not stop. Instead it headed out of the park. Both women were silent as the woman drove Mary home.

Mary was then sure that her boss was a lesbian and was wanting to rape her, but for some reason, changed her mind. Mary vowed never again to be found alone with the woman, realizing she was not safe with man or woman.

It was not long before she received a call at 11 p.m. from one of the salesmen in the business.

"I want you to go out with a salesman from out of town."

"No! I'm not going out with anyone."

He begged. She was adamant.

During the argument that ensued, Mary's landlady knocked and then banged on her door, demanding that Mary get rid of the man in her apartment.

Mary arrived to work the next morning and was immediately called into the office of the head administrator, a middle aged man in a brown suit she had little to do with except that he watched her daily through his glasses from behind a glass window—the barrier between her and him, but at close range of only fifteen feet from her desk.

"You're fired," he said.

"Why?"

"You know why. You are not working out here."

Mary left feeling dignified and glad. She was not going to compromise herself for a job. She walked away wondering about the other women in the office and now had a clue to what was going on with at least one woman.

Just when she was out of work again, Cisco phoned to say he was sending a moving truck and train tickets. The army was going to pay for it all. She was out of a job, pregnant, and the suite she had rented was in the basement of a house where the landlady was watching her every move and listening at her door.

Mary thought — *what the heck, I may as well be an army wife and see what happens. Maybe he is different as a soldier.*

Mary arrived at the army base across the county. The house he had rented was on the edge of a hill in a forest by a river that overlooked the army base. It immediately felt peaceful. She had only been there an hour and was sitting in her living room when Cisco came in and asked, "Do you want to meet my new girlfriend? She's outside." He laughed and went out.

Mary stood up, expecting a woman to walk in.

Cisco came back, holding a life-size cardboard picture of a woman. He laughed again. "Meet my girlfriend."

Mary was silent. Except for the lump in her stomach, she found it funny, but did not let him know.

To see a doctor, she had to go into town. Mary was always broke and never had enough money for taking the bus, so she would walk the eight miles with her baby in a carriage. She enjoyed the walk which was mostly just a walk in nature past other people's yards along the road that held all kinds of interesting things. She especially enjoyed the green yard where ducks ran around and swans enjoyed a pond. She wondered what it would be like to have such a stable life as these people in such a beautiful setting.

Cisco had not changed. Even though she was pregnant, he would suddenly be enraged for no apparent reason and beat her.

She gave birth to another son. This time there were no students watching. But, she was in her room after the birth and could hear the nurse on night duty yelling and swearing at the babies in the nursery. The nurse could not stand crying babies.

It was a relief to be released and get out of there with her four day old baby who already must have learned to dodge anger and swear words. Going home was another problem. Her husband could not wait for sex. As soon she entered the house and laid the baby down, he raped her even though she still had the mandatory cut and stitches after a vaginal birth.

Cisco was then hospitalized with ulcers. For a few days, Mary had peace to be home with her babies and not expect any violence. Then the army dismissed him for having ulcers.

Back to their home town. Now she was out of work and instead of getting another job right away with a new baby, she tried to rely on Cisco. That time was highlighted by having no winter boots for the cold and snow, and all her underwear had worn out, so she had no underpants. Meanwhile, he was using his income to rent hotel rooms for parties.

He decided to go to Hollywood to become a movie star. In a flash decision, he was gone again. Mary was content to be on her own. She had a job again and was managing. He returned just a quick as he had gone.

Mary packed her bags and left with her babies.

He had his friends follow her from work to her new apartment.

The landlady was too frightened to object as he did a surprise break and enter one evening. She was relieved to see Mary and the children leave with him.

That was the circus of the next few years. She left several times and was brought back under duress. She never knew who was following and keeping an eye on her.

Another child was born, regardless that she was now hating any physical contact with her husband and mentally imagined a wooden board in bed between her and him.

She was desperate to get out of the marriage and could not figure out how.

She could run home to the protection of her parents and admit her shame, but she was not yet willing to do so because of the turmoil it would cause in her parents' home when Cisco would fight to have her back.

It was the night as Mary laid in bed listening to the wind howl around the corners of the house, that she realized if Cisco came in drunk again and started to beat her or threaten the children, it might be life or death for one of them. She had come to the end of being in this situation. She was convinced if this kind of life continued, she would be dead or brain damaged beyond repair. She already had a dent in her skull after being sent through a wall.

She lay there in anticipation of him coming through the door and wondered what weapon she had to defend herself. She could think of nothing except for the knives in the kitchen, but the thought of a knife and blood was abhorrent, not something she could do. As scared as she was, it had come to fight or flight. Somehow it had to be flight.

The howling wind was especially loud when she heard the door open. She listened to him slowly make his way up the staircase to the second floor where the bedrooms were. He stopped at the doorway to the room where the boys were sleeping.

Mary leaped out of bed in fear that he may bother the boys. He saw Mary and reached toward her. She backed away. That infuriated him.

"Come here, woman!"

Mary ran past him and down the staircase in hopes that he would follow. He was behind her, demanding that she come to him.

She ran out of the house into the garden in her pyjamas and bare feet, hoping he would follow. He did.

She hid behind a bush. He wandered around briefly, grumbling as he looked for her.

Then he muttered something and found his way back to the house. Mary panicked. She was afraid for the children.

She found him face down, passed out on the sofa.

The next day, Mary was at work when life took a turn. She felt someone's presence. She looked up to see a man leaning over the row of filing cabinets by her desk, watching her.

Her first emotional response was that she did not like him.

He smiled. "I've been watching you. I'm going on a field trip to photograph flowers. Come with me."

"I don't know you."

"Ah, yes. I'm your husband."

"I have a husband."

"I know. I also know you want to have a different husband."

"How do you know that?"

"I've done my research. Play hooky. Come with me. I'm a photographer. My name is James. I work in the office down the hall. I've been watching you for a long time."

Mary wondered why she had never noticed him. She looked around the room to see who was watching or listening. It appeared that no one was interested.

She hesitated. She wondered why she disliked him at first glance because he was quite handsome with a great smile. It was an enticing idea to have an afternoon doing something entirely different and feeling free for a few hours. Her youthful desire for freedom kicked in.

"Okay. I'll do it."

Out on the hilltop, it was sunny with a chilly wind. She pulled her sweater closer around her body and watched with curiosity. She had never before seen a professional photographer working. She had never seen a camera like he was working with. She found herself attracted to him as he concentrated on flowers.

Back in the car he smiled at her. "How about more time? We can get to know each other at a motel."

Mary felt just fine being unfaithful to Cisco. She decided to simply enjoy herself.

James made comments about wanting to keep her forever in his pocket.

On the way home that same afternoon, James proposed that they live together immediately. He explained that he had a German Shepherd dog and hoped she would be okay with a dog. Mary thought that was a really good idea. This was her freedom flight and this time she felt success. She would have a man and a dog for protection.

Mary knew that Cisco had a fear of big dogs dating back to his childhood when he was out in the fields searching for gardens to raid for food and met with vicious dogs. She was convinced the dog would keep her and her children protected.

James rented an apartment the next day. While Cisco was at work one afternoon, Mary packed up and left the house with her children. This time, she knew it was forever. She felt sorry for Cisco to come home to an empty house, but she had to do it this way.

chapter three

Husband Two

Mary moved herself and children to her parents' home while she and James painted the new apartment. When she explained the situation to her parents in their garden, her father smiled and said, "Well, he's got to be better than the last one." And that was all.

Mary thought it was a good time to introduce her new partner to her parents, so he was invited to have supper with them. He was a bit late. Her parents, her children and Mary were all seated around the kitchen table when James knocked on the door and walked right in. Mary was shocked that his pants were sticking straight out ahead of him, leading the way. He had a penis that was protruding so far out that it was unavoidable for everyone to notice. Mary's breathing stopped, her eyes popped big and her face got red with embarrassment. Her parents pretended not to notice. Supper was served as though nothing was out of the ordinary.

They had been living in the apartment for only a few days when Cisco knocked on the door. He had found them. The dog leaped up and stood by the door. When there was no immediate answer, the door crashed open. Cisco was shocked to see a dog. His face turned white. He turned on his heels and walked away as fast as he could walk. It was ended. Cisco would never try that again.

Mary struggled with feelings of compassion. All she could see was the little boy suffering a war and facing a dog that he was afraid of. She struggled with the knowledge that she had stolen his children and he would forever know that they were gone. Nothing he had ever done to her could erase her compassion and caring for him as that hurt boy.

Trying to get a divorce turned into expensive letters passing back and forth with no resolution. As Mary watched her lawyer look intently at a picture on his desk of his wife and children as she was talking, she realized there was a big problem. It was a small enough town for her to know that he was having an affair with a woman other than his wife. She was trying to read his thoughts and imagined that he was afraid of divorce. She decided he would never work toward a divorce for her, but instead would continue an argument by letter and cash in on each letter. She simply gave up. Living common-law seemed better than feeling trapped in marriage anyway. In Mary's mind, common-law meant two people really wanted to be together rather than being tied by law. She was happy and her children were handling the new arrangement very well. She was free.

Life seemed good until the day James suggested a babysitter that lived in another suite in the same building. That was fine with Mary. The woman was sort of their same age and seemed nice enough, although Mary never really had a chance to get to know her. She came and went within seconds of Mary leaving and coming.

James was out of work. His female boss had found out about him living with Mary, a married woman, and fired him. He set up a photography studio in the apartment and was home while Mary was out working.

The woman suddenly quit without notice and avoided Mary. In fact, Mary never saw her again even though she lived in the same building. Mary asked James why. He just shrugged. Because of the veil of secrecy that both the woman and James seemed to be in, Mary suspected that James may have tried a sexual advance and the woman rejected him.

It was Jame's idea that they start a Bohemian style coffee house. It would be the first in the city or even the whole countryside for hundreds of miles. Mary had jumped out of working for the government and into the Arts Board. She felt closer to musicians and artists than to the business community she had been in for so long.

The warehouse rented for the coffee house had been a motor vehicle service outlet. It came with an out-of-body man who showed himself to people occasionally. It seemed to be known that he had worked in the shop and did not leave when he died. It seemed that he was curious to see what was going on. Strangely, no one was afraid of him. They just went about their business, knowing there was a spirit around. He was somehow comforting.

James organized a few well seasoned artists who already were successfully supporting themselves with their artistic endeavours. They were excited about the coffee house and were volunteering their time to help in the renovations. One accomplished artist came to the Art Board to talk with Mary. He wanted to see what she had to show him of her own work. She did not have any with her, but she got so excited at his interest that she backed into her own desk and fell backward onto it. They both laughed. She enjoyed her own comedy.

The volunteers helped to make a kitchen and built a few dividing walls and a stage to organize the place.

Working along with the builders, Mary took on the dirty work and cleaned the several filthy bathroom stalls. Then she renovated a long wall by putting up chicken wire with paper mache and flour glue to build a wall looking like it was made of stone and painted it white. She sewed red and white checkered table cloths.

Mary's father built round wooden tables with three legs at his own expense as his contribution and sign of approval. The three legged tables were because of the uneven cement floor. He said three legs would keep them stable — and they did. Mary once again admired her father's knowledge and capabilities of the everyday things that mattered.

They hired a potter to make special cups that were a special signature for the coffee house.

Mary and James scoured all the second hand shops for wooden kitchen chairs. They were all different and when painted gave a uniform, artsy, matching atmosphere around the checkered table cloths with candle holders on top.

Mary was the financial backer to the whole project except for her father's input.

Opening evening, students and staff from the university and arts community lined up along the street to enter. It was a success even before the doors opened.

From then on, every evening was filled with music on the small stage at one end of the room and all the tables and chairs were filled with people. Coffee and snacks were served non-stop.

One night a week, Mary made a dinner of cabbage rolls and delivered it to the coffee house for serving to whoever wanted dinner. Friday night was folk music. Saturday nights was jazz, and so on—all live music. Every night was filled with something.

It was an oasis of peace for some people and a place to work out mental and emotional distress for others.

James found his niche in being the boss. Mary was busy with her children and working at the Arts Board to support home and coffee house financially. She would appear occasionally, trusting James to run the business.

One evening, Mary arrived and James was not in the coffee house.

The waiter approached her. The look in his eyes told her it was bad news.

"I just discovered that someone stole all the cash out of the register."

"Oh, no! Where's James?"

"He's out."

"Do you know where he's gone? Where is the waitress?"

"I don't know where he's gone. He went with the waitress. I'm here alone, trying to serve and watch the cash register at the same time."

Mary looked toward the cash register in an alcove by the dimly lit door. It would be easy for someone leaving to take the cash if no one was looking after it.

Mary was not sure how to behave in the moment she knew James had taken off with the waitress. She stood there looking around at the people and wondering who knew what was going on. Running through her head was the thought that the waitress was a young, sort of dumpy female and he was choosing to be with her.

"Okay," she said. "Just carry on the best you can for now. I'm sorry, but I need to get back to my children. I can't stay."

The waiter rushed back to the kitchen.

Mary went home and stood in front of a painting on the living room wall. It was a large portrait that she had painted on canvas of James and herself as a loving couple. She took the painting off the wall and went to the kitchen with it. She slashed it with a knife down the middle between herself and James.

Mary was glad the babysitter had fallen asleep and not wakened to see the drama. In a frenzy, she rushed out into the snow with the slashed painting and headed for the coffee house.

At the coffee house, heads turned in her direction as she stood at the entrance with the slashed painting.

Normally, everyone would not notice someone coming and going, but now there was a dumbfounded pause that pervaded the room. All eyes were on her as everyone waited for her to do something. She did not know what to do and never felt more stupid in her life.

Mary said to the waiter, "Give this to James."

She set it down against the wall and left everyone with their mouths open.

After being sure that her children were sleeping, Mary laid down in bed. She was wide-eyed, watching the clock that ticked loudly.

She wondered — *what do I do now? — alone with a ticking clock — an unfaithful husband — three children — what do I do next and not be vulnerable to Cisco in any move?*

Suddenly, Mary felt the sensation of vibration that started low in feel and sound and went high and faster in feel with sound. It was familiar. She remembered often feeling the vibration in her childhood just before she fell asleep. Her body rocked from side to side on the inside of her body. With a whoosh she slid upward and out of her body through her head. Even though there was a wall at her head, it was no longer solid and she slid through it as though it was not there. She looked at her silver cord attached from her astral body to her physical body at the belly. She hovered over her physical body that was now feeling every thread in the sheets as though magnified millions of times. Mary began traveling away from her physical body, still aware of the silver cord attaching her to her body. She quickly found herself in a dimly lit tunnel with light at the far end. Along the way, there were round blob kind of beings watching her as she traveled— some reaching out, beckoning and pleading for her to stay and help. She paused, not knowing how to help. As

she moved toward the light, the blobs were left behind. Then, in fear of losing her body, she looked to see if she was still attached to her silver cord. Suddenly, her silver cord sprung her back into her body.

To make sure she was alive, Mary's hands felt her body up and down, pausing on her belly button. She was again aware of the clock ticking loudly. She was really back in her room.

She talked out loud just to hear her voice. "It's real! The silver cord is real! It keeps us safe! As a kid, the same vibrations happened to me nightly before I fell asleep. I was astral travelling! I understand now."

She could hear the door open. She stared at the clock. It said 3:30. She rolled over, pretending to be sleeping.

In the morning, she studied herself in the bathroom mirror, looking for clues of why James was unfaithful. She knew this was not his first time. She reasoned that this time seemed worse because the coffee house crowd knew. She decided her face was not unattractive because each of her features was correctly in place. Her body? She enjoyed a healthy, elastic body, inside and out. No matter how many times she thought she would explode with a pregnancy, she had marvelled that like magic, her body always sprung back into its original form quickly. She had inherited good genes. She knew that she had a zest for life, never depressed or bored. She could see nothing unattractive. On the other hand, she analyzed James for a minute and knew he had a history of being unfaithful to his former wife long before

Mary met him. She thought how he hid in the bathroom when it was time for bed. She soon knew that it was because he had a hard time keeping up with her libido. She thought he needed to prowl for conquests to prove something to himself.

As Mary gazed into the mirror, she felt cheated of love. She decided his behaviour could and would affect her health. She had enough and needed to do something about it.

Mary was too upset to argue. She brooded silently. She needed to consider her children and their needs, so it was important to plan a way out without another upheaval for the children. Getting out of another relationship was a problem that she dreaded explaining to her parents. Meanwhile, James offered no explanation, thinking he had gotten off easily.

Then there were symptoms Mary had never seen or heard of before. The doctor said it was Gonorreah. Now, she felt that she was dirty, damaged goods with a venereal disease.

With a diagnosis of a venereal disease, James panicked. That same evening, James brought a small army to the house to combat a break-up. Four men from the regular coffee house patrons tried to convince Mary that James needed another chance because it was usually women at fault for situations like this one; they meant all women — the woman enticing a man and the woman whose man was unfaithful. In other words, they wanted to abolish all blame for men's behaviour.

Mary could not go along with their version of blame. In her quiet way, Mary listened, but was thinking these men were not her friends.

Seeing her reluctance to believe them, James proposed a solution. "Let's start over. Let's move a long way away and start over."

Mary was surprised. "I don't see how that will change anything between us."

"Let's do it. I promise to be faithful."

"Why do you want to be with me?"

"You are great to be with — to live with. I chose you to live with. I don't want to live with another woman."

"Why would you jeopardize our relationship then?"

"I was drawn in … kind of like I was magnetized … I mean maybe like hypnotized."

"How could you? I work to pay her wages. I work all week to pay the bills for this home, the coffee house, and babysitters so that I can go to work. Meanwhile, you screw around at leisure … not only the waitress, but any woman I make friends with and even my babysitters while I am at work. I found a bra in the laundry basket just last week … not mine. I know who it belongs to. I heard her running out the back door when I came home through the front door. You had to ditch the bra. I just didn't tell you that I know."

James was silent, not knowing how to respond.

Mary was looking intently at him. She could see a handsome man, but inner beauty was missing. He was a liar and a cheat. She was thinking back to the first time she saw him and realized that intuition was telling her that she did not like him. She was blaming herself now for ignoring her wiser self. She had traded one quandary for another and there had been no real love in either relationship.

Instead of going to work the next morning, Mary walked to the park to think. She was seeing the world as grey, lacking light.

Everything was covered with hoarfrost. As the sun came out between clouds, the hoarfrost covering trees glistened with light. The world around her and her own inner world suddenly was bright. She could feel her heart leap with hope and happiness in the sparkling world where she had children to think about and care for.

Standing in all the light, Mary thought about staying in this place versus moving and starting over. The idea of starting over in a totally new place appealed to her. The idea of starting a new life by going back to school and becoming a nurse also appealed to her.

Mary went back to talk to James about a separation. She reasoned, "I can't see anything wrong with me. My face and my body are in proper places. My body needs sex. My heart needs love. I am cheated of all of that because of you. Why?"

He responded, "You're a mother ... so pure ... so right ... so ... uh, beautiful. She is so trampy. I guess, I was attracted to trampy."

"You are so ... I can't think of a word." Mary was stuck for words. "I just need to separate."

James did not give up. He was persuasive, promising all sorts of behaviour changes. He asked her to visit the Jesuit priest who had been a regular patron of the coffee house.

The priest convinced Mary that working on the relationship was the best way to go forward.

Mary looked at a map with James. They imagined life by going east or west. East won for no particular reason.

Mary watched as her softly, gleaming oak dining room suite was being carried out of the house, piece by piece. Table, buffet, china cabinet, chairs passed by her. The dishes her parents had given her for Christmas. She was wondering how stupid she could be.

James approached her. "You are proving your wonderfulness and that you forgive us."

James had convinced her to give her dining room suite to the waitress he had been unfaithful with. According to James, Mary was cleaning her soul. She turned away from James in disbelief and disgust for his way of thinking that it was somehow her debt to pay. She had agreed instead of giving the furniture to her sister and she felt awful about it.

An overwhelming sadness overtook Mary as she watched her mother's armoire go out the door. It had been a gift to her from her father and now it had been Mary's.

She was feeling sorry for agreeing to go away, to be taking her children away from family Sunday dinners at her parents' house. She was having pangs of guilt that her parents would no longer hear the laughter of their grandchildren and that her children were losing their grandparents all because James was running away from himself and she had agreed to go with him.

Spring had sprung and the weather was warm. Children and their dog were in the back seat, enjoying the excitement of the trip. The old car had a wooden box on top, holding their total belongings. It held minimal clothing, bedding, a few dishes and cooking pots and pans. Mary had managed to hang onto her favourite Beethoven record and her manuscript and notes of her first attempt to write a book. She also held onto the kids' small record player that her parents had given to the kids at Christmas and she played Mozart and Beethoven on it for them daily. Everything else had been left behind. The coffee house had been for sale to a patron who wanted it. Even though it had been all legalized in a lawyer's office, Mary knew she would never collect the money owed. She knew it was another giveaway.

Mary had been enjoying the green forest around the north side of the Great Lakes when a realization came over her that caused her to shudder uncontrollably. It was an overwhelming awareness that she did not want to grow old with James, and for sure, she never wanted to live with him in this kind of wilderness. She was thinking that if you truly love someone, you would live anywhere with that person, even in a tent. She shuddered again at the thought of living alone with this man anywhere but especially in this wilderness.

Unknown to Mary at the time, she was having real foreknowledge because later in life, James would return to live in this exact area. He would live his life to its end here and she would not be with him.

Hundreds of miles away, they set up camp for a while on a beach by a small lake. Mary was surprised that James had all the training from his Airforce days to set up camp with all the amenities needed. He built a table out of tree branches for her to cook on. He dug a pit and built an oven in the sand. He built an outhouse with a seat for a toilet where a person could sit in private comfort. He built a bouncy bed in the tent out of young tree bows.

Mary was able to cook and bake bread and pans of gingerbread each day in comfort. In the brief contentment of the place, Mary became pregnant again.

Mary and the children were playing in the shallow water of the lake by their campsite. She took a small swim close to the children, but a little farther out in deeper water. She saw James approach her from underwater and grab her legs. She thought he was playing, so she kicked and got loose and swam back to shore.

At the shore she mentioned that he had grabbed her legs and she got free. She laughed.

"I was no where near you. I did not grab your legs," he denied.

This was shocking. She had seen him clearly and thought he was playing. Now she was with someone who denied grabbing her legs under water. She wondered — *what was he trying to do — would he have drowned me with my children nearby?*

She was confused, wondering — *why did he want to stay together if he also wants to harm me?*

The only thing that had changed was that she was pregnant. Now she felt unsafe.

While still on the beach after the incident, Mary had a lucid dream:

A giant golden eagle larger than Mary washed her in a stream of clear water.

She thought it meant that something new and different was about to happen.

They reached their destination and found a small apartment over a garage. There, Mary had a second lucid dream:

A nun with dark eyes came to her and told that she would give birth to a daughter—the daughter would leave the family at a young age and never return—there would be nothing Mary or anyone could do to change that.

Mary was so disturbed by the dream and seemingly threatening nature of that dream that she slept in her clothes for many nights.

After a while, she dismissed the second dream and then simply forgot it.

Mary found a job as secretary in a science lab. James stayed home to look after the children and start a photography retouching business in the new city.

Mary woke up hemorrhaging blood. She was having a miscarriage. She lost a tiny fetus in her bathroom. Later in the day, she was relaxing while James happily celebrated.

When morning sickness continued, she saw a doctor who proclaimed she was pregnant. She had lost a twin but still had a viable pregnancy.

chapter four

The Teaching

Mary was in her last trimester of pregnancy when the telephone rang. It was an invitation to attend a meeting with a Buddhist monk new in town. It seemed interesting even though neither she or James had any experience with Buddhism. Their only dabbling in eastern thought was a bit of Zen after a public lecture by Alan Watts and discussions with people at the coffee house.

A Buddhist monk in saffron robes and holding sandalwood beads sat on a chair in meditation. The only furniture in the room was his chair, so Mary sat on a gleaming wood floor with a small group of people facing him. They watched intently in anticipation of — they knew not what.

Some people tried to meditate but uneven breathing and clearing of throats cut into the stillness permeating the room.

The monk opened his eyes and looked intently at each person.

He spoke. "Welcome. You have come to learn. You will learn. You shall call me 'Bhikhu' meaning 'teacher'. You have come to see. You will see. First, let me set some of you straight. We do not use what you will learn for selfish reasons. Remember that. I will use many devious methods to teach you and you will learn, despite yourselves. I will teach by the left-hand Tantra where necessary. But, we do not resort to such lowly devises as seances and Ouija Boards. None of that! You will prepare yourself for life after life. There is no death. Your present delusion is your flesh and bones, your ties which are all delusions. You belong to no one and no one belongs to you. You cannot own another person."

Mary was having trouble hearing all this because she was pregnant with raging hormones of wanting to love and belong to someone who loved her. She wanted to know safety in being able to express love in every way unabashedly. She wanted her baby to belong to her. She knew she had none of that now, but she wanted it.

The monk was still speaking. "You must clear your minds and you will clear your lives. You must meditate. You will meditate. This is the way. You cannot do any clearing by filling yourself with intellectual discussion of the scriptures. We will do some intellectual study but we will meditate."

Mary was thinking how James liked to pretend to be the wise one in all conversations and here he was listening. She tried to be invisible as the monk was again looking at each person.

"I will see each of you privately. You will make appointments with me. Now I will teach you to meditate."

As the evening went on, Mary was convinced she would not return.

On the walk home, James announced that he had found his man.

Even though Mary had not thought of returning, she found herself sitting in front of the monk one afternoon. She wanted to talk about astral travel. She had never talked to anyone about it before.

He was saying to her, "You need to learn control."

They sat in silence for a few minutes. Then he continued, "Intuition is your receiving instrument. Intuition is your guidance. Thoughts vibrate eternally in the cosmos. You are a sender and a receiver. We all are. Some people are deaf and blind even though they have ears and eyes. They are not open to the fine-tuning. We are like radios sending and receiving. People become indignant about your kind of experience out of fear and that's why you have had trouble talking about what is going on with you. What they do not see and hear or touch, they believe is invalid, while all they have to do is open their minds, listen with their inner being … their true selves, and see beyond their noses. What is inside is outside. Look to nature for the secrets of the universe."

They sat in silence again.

He spoke again, "You are ready for more. You must meditate. Will you be our coordinator of the meditation centre?"

"What meditation centre?"

"We will have one soon. There will be many monks and nuns over time. There will be hundreds of people meditating. You shall see."

"When?"

"Very soon. This is January … I think by March."

"I have children."

"Children will be good for the meditator. They will not lose their way so easily." He paused and then went on, "Your job will not be easy. You will live in poverty. You will give of yourself in service of others. You will gain more than by meditation."

"Ha. Well, what's different? Sorry, I just thought this sounds like what I've been doing. I'll be giving birth in March."

"I know. You'll be okay. … When you are ready."

Meditation was not so simple. There had been a warning about itches and aches developing to distract. They happened, followed by twitching. Mary had all of them. That was followed by an attempt to control the mind that wanted to wander. Mary was realizing how totally out of control her mind had been. It conjured up people's faces and actions and her emotions rose. Problems of relationships, problems of daily living, responsibilities all refused to let Mary get on with the peace expected in meditation.

Bhikhu told the group in another meeting, "Learn control by watching. Observe how your mind works, then you will learn control. You must cut through your ego. This is all delusion. Your ego thinks it is real. Your ego keeps you from knowing what is real. Why suffer any longer? You can do it … you can know complete awareness. You must use your powers with discrimination. If you use power selfishly or to destroy others, your power will turn on you and destroy you."

He pulled out a deck of Tarot cards from under his robe. He held up the thirteenth Arcana card of Death.

"You must know this card, understand the meaning of this card. At first glance this looks like death in the form of a skeleton wielding a scythe. Death and destruction! Look closer. This is destruction followed by change. There is new growth below his feet. As he reaps, new growth appears. Transformation ... renewal ... rebirth. This card does not mean death; it means change, regeneration of the soul and eternal life. The number thirteen is not unlucky. It is a number that will destroy the user if it is used selfishly. If used unselfishly, it brings new life."

He then held up the Fool card. "Most of you are now like the Fool. You are stepping off the edge of the cliff, looking upward, unaware of what is beneath your feet. You carry your stored up universal knowledge on the end of a stick loftily over a shoulder. Some of you might use it like a chip on your shoulder to prove your wisdom to others."

He paused and leaned forward. "You know not what you are getting into. The Fool is youthful innocence about to enter a supreme adventure."

He paused again and looked at each person.

"You must keep your feet on the ground even though your head is in the clouds. Balance. You must keep balance."

Mary gave birth to a girl at the end of March, just as land had been purchased and the meditation centre was born.

It was quite a blow to Jame's ego when Mary was sent out to the center ahead of him. He was told by Bhikhu to stay home and babysit. Mary thought it quite a trick to play on the man who liked to think he was superior and all knowing.

Two cars traveled together. Mary was in Bhikhu's car which traveled fast. They stopped at a picture-book scene of hilly green fields surrounded by groves of trees. On exploration there was a small lake with beavers. There was one old, dilapidated log cabin on the property and a pretty water well made of stone that was dry with a dead porcupine at the bottom.

Mary entered the log house, trying to visualize being at home in it with her family. The floors had holes. The log walls had large gaps so that the outside could be viewed between the logs. The outside weather had run through the house for years. There was no electricity, no running water, no bathroom. There was an area upstairs divided in two for bedrooms that seemed cleaner and in better shape than the rest of the house. She wondered what she was getting herself into.

While other people were still exploring the acres, Mary sat in a small grove near the house. She was feeling peaceful and happy. Then, something opposite of her enjoyment seemed to settle around her. It was as though a dark shadow had emerged out of a crack. She had only a glimmer of it and could not exactly see the dark shadow. A foreboding came over her. It was familiar somehow. She wondered if she was having Déjà vu. She wondered if she had dreamt the event or had she seen this place in a dream. The familiarity of the place convinced her that long ago she had dreamed of this place, but the more she tried to remember, the more it closed down until it was only a feeling.

It was Jame's turn to go to the meditation centre. He was one of a working group to renovate the cabin. A car drove up to the house to pick him up with a married couple in the front seats and a woman in the back seat.

James was in a hurry to get out of the house before Mary realized who was in the car. Mary stood in the doorway holding her baby, shocked to see the woman waiting for James.

"You're going with her?" Mary asked.

"We're going to work at the centre. That's all! You had your day, now it's my turn."

"You're going to sleep with her?"

"Don't worry. We'll be in the same tent, but we'll be in separate sleeping bags."

James ran to the car to avoid any more questions. The car sped off.

Mary watched the car disappear down the street. It was the woman who had angrily painted a picture with black scribbles while looking at Mary in the painting session people had been invited to in the studio of a sculptor. The woman had seemed unhinged to Mary and for some reason, she did not like Mary. Now Mary knew why.

It was decided to give up the rented house in the city so that James could live at the centre while working there. Mary and the children would board a train and go home to her parents' home until the log cabin was ready for them.

Going home to her parents was a relief and difficult at the same time. She was getting away from the turmoil James was now presenting. Somehow she needed to explain to her parents what was lying ahead.

Mary's father expressed his worry that she was taking his grandchildren into a cult. She tried to convince him that it was not a cult and that she would have free will all the time and could leave if things were not right for her and the children. Over the month, her father could not be convinced, progressing into anger about the situation. Mary wanted to leave just to get away from her father who had always tried to protect her.

It was time to board the train again and head back even though James wanted her to stay longer and told her so.

On arrival, Bhikhu's two right hand men came to get the family from the train station. James was not there. The information was that a week of meditation had already started, so there were dozens of people on the grounds, in tents somewhere among the trees.

On arrival at the centre, James was missing. It was certainly not the greeting Mary expected.

The family was escorted into the cabin. Mary was amazed at the interior. There was new flooring—bare cement, but new. Her large table sat in the center of the large kitchen with a dozen chairs around it. Her refrigerator from the city was against the wall and hooked up to electricity which was minimal. She was glad to see one electrical light bulb in the room. Against the far wall stood a wood-burning stove with a large yellow lion painted on the back-splash over the cook-top and under the warming shelf. There was one green cupboard. Mary opened it and found her dishes and pots and pans.

The children meanwhile, had been racing through the rest of the house, cheering loudly.

As the men who delivered the family to the centre were leaving, an excited woman came rushing in.

"Ssshh! Ssshh!"

Mary was surprised. "What's the matter?"

"There are meditators out there in tents You'll disturb them."

The woman turned and disappeared just as Bhikhu walked in.

"Welcome!" his voice boomed and traveled out the open windows and doorway. "I'm glad you made it. Hi, kids." He then launched into tousles and minor wrestling with the children. Noise escalated in hollers and laughing.

"Want to learn some Aikido?" he asked.

They launched into a few Aikido moves with lots of noise.

Bhikhu went out just as a car arrived and a small man, one of the original starting group dropped three boxes of food on the table. He said, "I've worked out the menu. It's over there on the cupboard."

Mary examined the food in the boxes and asked, "How long is this food to last and for how many people?"

He answered, "Thirty people. They'll be here all week."

"Thirty people? All week?"

"Oh, I've worked it all out. The menu is on the cupboard counter."

As Mary read the menu and looked into the boxes, the man disappeared.

Mary was holding her baby outside the cabin, wondering which way the Bhikhu went. A kind looking woman approached, "Can I hold your baby a moment?"

"Hi. I'm Mary. Yes. I need to talk with the Bhikhu. Do you know how I can find him?"

"That way," she pointed. "I'll look after the baby if you like while you talk to him."

Gratefully, Mary took off to find him. She approached the hill with a large orange tent on top. There was a screened area where the Bhikhu sat, giving counsel to students. Mary stood behind a young man to wait her turn.

He introduced himself. "Hi, I'm Peter. You must be Mary. You going to live here?"

"Yes and yes."

A student was leaving the orange tent, followed by the Bhikhu who stood outside the tent with his hands on his hips and looking down the hill at Peter.

He chanted, "Peter, Peter, pumpkin eater, had a wife and couldn't keep her."

Peter headed up the hill and into the screened area. Mary could watch but not hear.

Peter came down the hill with a bewildered look on his face. As he approached Mary, he shook his head and paused a moment. "How did he know I have a letter in my pocket from my girlfriend ... a letter saying goodbye?"

"You mean a wife you couldn't keep?"

"You got it!"

As Peter walked on, Mary headed up the hill. The tent was glowing like being inside a brilliant orange jewel. Bhikhu was seated in a chair in all the glow. He offered her a chair.

Mary took a deep breath and launched in. "The food ... there's not enough. If I'm to cook, I want to also plan the menu. It's not got enough protein. Some days, it's practically got none. I don't think that man knows what he's doing. I need to make my own menus. Those people are going to be starved after a week. Three small boxes of food, two pounds of cheese, two dozen eggs for more than thirty people ... for a week!"

A glimmer of annoyance crossed Bhikhu's eyes, but he spoke softly. "He needs to do that job. He's working out his karma."

"But how can I manage?"

"I never said your job would be easy."

Bhikhu rose from his chair and walked to the doorway, dismissing Mary.

She needed to think. Instead of going back to the cabin, she walked along the dirt road outside the meditation centre, kicking small stones to skip along the dirt. She was going over the problems of looking after groups of people with no running water, no bathroom, not enough food, only two light bulbs on the main floor and none in the bedrooms upstairs, and being bossed around by strangers. She wondered how she could care for her own children here.

She found a small path into the forest and followed it. She was wondering what possessed her to come here and have to deal with other people's karma. She thought this was the third major mistake of her life—when would she get wise and quit making bad mistakes, and start making solutions?

The forest was quiet with life. She breathed it in and began to calm down.

James sauntered out of somewhere. She did not see where. "Hey, what are you doing out here?" he asked.

"Thinking. What are you doing here?"

James swung his arms around. "Just looking over the dead wood for firewood. Look, there's lots of old logs fallen. If we run out of that, there's plenty of wood in the stands to go on for years."

"But it won't last forever. I worry about trees being used up. What then?"

"Don't worry your head about those things. Hey, while you're here, I'll show you the spring where we get the water. You know, there's no water in the well. It's dry. We cleaned it but it's still dry."

"Yes, I know it's dry."

James led Mary a short distance along the narrow path through the trees. They came upon a tiny spring that bubbled up out of the earth into a small rock lined pool of crystal clear water. Excess water streamed on through the woods.

"You can't find better water than this anywhere." James said.

Mary was thinking that this was the first thing they shared in a long time. Looking at his face, mixed feelings welled up. She wanted to share life, love, and to be young with someone, not just to be responsible and separate. She was wishing for real love beside the spring. She thought about her first husband always seeing her as an optimist because she always told him that tomorrow would be better. And here she was believing in tomorrow again.

That evening, the children were in bed and Mary was cleaning the kitchen. She heard footsteps approaching the cabin. The door swung open and there stood the Bhikhu with mischief in his eyes.

"Well, what's for a bedtime snack?"

"A snack?"

He sat on a chair by the side-table near the door as though waiting for a snack.

He said, "I think some of that cheese with bread and tea would do just fine."

"Oh, yes. Sure. Uh, I'll get it," Mary responded.

"How are the children?"

"I guess they're okay. They're sleeping."

"Feed them well. They are growing boys and girls. They need nourishment."

Bhikhu was enjoying his evening snack and small talk with Mary as she continued cleaning the kitchen. Then he asked innocently, "What's for breakfast?"

Mary reached for the prepared menu paper.

He interrupted, "I'm homesick for a good breakfast of salt eggs and saffron rice."

"Salt eggs and saffron rice? Oh, I don't think that's written here at all. I don't even know how to make it."

"I'll show you. Where are the eggs and brown rice?"

He got up and joined Mary in the cooking area by the stove as she brought out the eggs and brown rice. Together, they boiled water for the salt brine. They boiled all the eggs and peeled them. Then they laid the eggs in the salt brine.

Bhikhu explained, "They'll be ready by morning. A good Tai breakfast. Now in the morning we will make the rice. I'll be here at 6:30."

He disappeared into the night, leaving Mary looking at the eggs and with a lot to think about—he had just boiled all the eggs in the house and put them in salt brine for breakfast. Those eggs would throw the menu off for the whole week. The menu was now useless.

Of course, that's it, she thought. *He is showing me how to deal with it all—I must accept the gracious help of the menu man, but I must do what I have to do to make my own job work—and to make my own life work—I don't have to be ruled by that other man. Snacks? Right! The monk is telling me the kids can have snacks and I should not feel guilty about giving my children special care. How right!*

The meditators went back to the city after that first week. From then on there were often thirty or more guests on weekends. Mary never knew who or how many people would arrive, nor how long they would stay.

The days were filled with baking bread and biscuits, cooking meals for what seemed like endless people in weeks of meditation and weekend visitors. It was up to Mary to figure out how to keep the food supply happening because no one paid their way. Except for a few donations of food, it was a free for all.

There was endless piles of dishes to wash. People loved outdoor work, but no one offered to help in the kitchen. People thought they were there as guests to be taken care of. Rumors of jealousies drifted back to Mary. It seemed a few women were jealous of Mary's job, so she decided to give the kitchen over to those women on a weekend and Mary would only be there to act as a guide. She wanted the women to see how hard it was with no facilities and serving people like them on top of it each weekend. James' woman friend refused to do any work in the kitchen while she stuck close to him outdoors all weekend. Meanwhile, Mary set up washtubs outside the cabin and scrubbed clothes by hand all weekend.

After the weekend of hard labor, rumors of jealousy appeared to stop and the women did not return to the kitchen.

After that weekend, Mary wondered if she was there to learn about her own low tolerance of other people's capabilities, or was she there to learn tolerance of their lack of capabilities. She thought, maybe she was there to learn tolerance of society in general—was she here to learn or to teach? It beat her. She just wanted to be alone for a while. She was not getting paid for hard work and insults.

chapter five

Water

L imited water brought by men willing to go and get it meant that scrubbing clothes and diapers in a washtub and using a scrub board was a problem because cooking and washing dishes always took precedent.

There came the day when the lack of water became such an issue that a guest offered whiskey barrels to be filled with water. Mary was delighted as barrels with taps sat in the kitchen and she had 'almost' running water for a while.

A few weeks after the arrival of the barrels, guests became ill with upset stomachs after a visit the centre. A message was relayed to Mary that she was to blame because she must have cooked their food on that weekend with wrong thoughts.

When that news got back to Mary, she thought it was plain stupid. She was insulted.

On investigation, it turned out the barrels had grown a mold that made the barrels useless and caused people to have stomach problems.

Now Mary was reduced to using water collected from rain that drained from the roof into her metal washtub outside her door. Even though James and other men, who now had taken on permanent residency because they simply did not leave, could have brought water from the stream, there often was none.

She had enjoyed the presence of a little mouse with big ears that ran along the logs in her bedroom. He looked like Mickey Mouse and for that reason, he was an acceptable entertainment each morning. When she mentioned the mouse had not been seen in a while, one of the men said it had drowned in the water outside the door and he had removed it. Meanwhile, Mary had been using the water for her family and everything else. This made her feel sick. She wondered how these men could have allowed her to keep using the water.

A young woman with a long ponytail came with a bag under her arm one weekend.

"Here are a few of my clothes. I thought you might like them."

"Thanks." Mary was pleased because she needed a few changes that suited this job.

In her bedroom the next morning, Mary found a nice pair of rust colored corduroy slacks and tried them on. They fit. She was pleased. She started to walk across the room and stopped suddenly. She felt Eric and this woman having sex. She gulped and shuddered. Still wearing the slacks, she continued down the stairs. She was putting wood in the cooking stove to start the breakfast when the woman came into the kitchen from the outside. She walked up to Mary and tried to compliment her for wearing the slacks.

"Morning! They fit you nicely."

Mary turned to face her and very quietly said, "Morning. Have you had sex with James?"

The woman answered in a surprisingly matter of fact way, "Yes."

"Where? When?"

"He comes to my tent."

Mary said no more. She continued her work, realizing that wearing other people's clothing was actually dangerous for her. She did not want to wear another person's life. Mary had the experience more than once that when she sat on a chair another person had just left, she could know what the person was thinking while sitting there; often the thoughts were different than the ongoing conversation — often the thoughts were hidden criticism. She was too sensitive and could pick up knowledge from objects, water, and through air because everything holds energy. Empty space of air is not empty. Mary vowed never to wear second hand clothes again.

Mary had more critical problems. Water was the most ongoing critical problem. Mary had reached desperation. She was burning with the insult that she was to blame for gastric problems. She was thinking — *there is an old Chinese saying: If a thousand people say a foolish thing, it is still foolish. I say: If one person says a truth, it is still a truth.*

It was evening when she went out to have a talk with the well. She looked into it. It was still completely dry — not even a drop of water on the stone bottom.

She begged, "Please well, I need water. If you give me water, I'll plant flowers all around you."

Every morning Mary had been in the habit of stopping at the window above the staircase to look at the countryside and marvel that she lived in such a beautiful place. The morning after talking to the well, as she gazed out, she could see that there was water on the ground around the well. She ran out to see it close up. Approaching the well, she saw that the well was so full of water that it overflowed. Water was surrounding the well in a flood over the ground. It had not even rained. The weather had been completely dry for many days.

Feeling the supernatural force of what was happening, she spoke to the well again. "Thank you. Thank you for all the water. But, I cannot get near enough to use your water because there is too much. I need to have water this far from the top."

She showed a measurement with her hands in the air of approximately two feet.

Mary was feeling a presence and felt she was talking to a real person.

She kept it all a secret, not willing to have anyone interfere with what was happening for her, and luckily for her, no one seemed to notice.

The very next morning, she rushed to her window and was delighted to see the water was still there. It was still true! She could see that the water was lower in the well. She dashed down the stairs and out to the well.

This time, she was able to walk up close on dry ground that somehow had dried over a few hours. The water in the well was exactly two feet below the top of the stone wall. There was debris floating on top and seemed to be throughout the water as deep as she could see.

Mary spoke to the well again. "Thank you, well, for all the water and thank you for the depth exactly as I asked for. But, I need clean water. I need you to be clean enough to drink."

Again, there was a feeling of a presence other than herself.

The next morning she stood looking into the well. The water looked completely clean and clear. There was not a spec of dirt, it was a perfect level and the ground was dry around it.

Mary thanked the well and whoever, whatever the energy was present to help her with water. She believed more than ever in the tangible power of the unseen world. The whole thing was unbelievable but the proof was right in the well in front of everyone.

The well water was sent for testing. It proved to be absolutely pure and clean. Mary's water problems were over.

Then, another problem arose. The man who had taken a drowned mouse out the rain water and allowed Mary to continue using it, could not draw water from the well. His pail stayed upright. No matter how he tried, his pail would not turn over to fill with water. He was really upset.

One evening, a group of new people who were visiting from the city were sitting around the kitchen table and heard from the guy who could not get water about how his pail would not turn over. A young man from the group decided to go and try his luck to get some water out of the well. His pail would not fill with water. He came screaming back to the kitchen.

"That well is witched! I can't get water. The pail won't turn over."

"I'll go." Mary offered.

She came back with water.

The young man's girlfriend got upset. "You're a witch!" she shouted at Mary.

Everyone was silently watching for Mary's reaction.

Mary responded, "I prefer to think of water as a gift from the Cosmos. I certainly am not a witch. Maybe I am simply a water diviner like my father. He could find water anywhere and did for many farmers on the prairies. My father taught me how to divine water."

She thought she had told them too much and that her father had divined water with willow twigs, not the way this well gave water, but Mary thought the people in the room would not know the difference anyway.

Never-the-less, people enjoyed the water now in abundance but looked at Mary with suspicion because the whole situation was so unbelievable.

Mary wondered what the problem was because the water in the well was tangible and however it happened, could they not just accept it?

There seemed to be no end of riddles. Bhikhu was having his evening tea and snack at the side table as he watched Mary sterilizing baby bottles in a large pot over the hot stove. She laid out clean cloths in the centre of his table and was lifting hot bottles out of the steaming pot with her bare finger tips, carrying them one by one across the room to set them on the cloth.

Bhikhu asked, "Do you not burn yourself doing that?"

Mary laughed and joked, "Hah, when one is spiritual, one does not burn self."

"Oh." He sipped his tea. "Hmm … you think so?"

He got up and went out into the night.

Mary turned back to the stove and realized it needed wood. She lifted a stove-top circular covering plate and picked up a piece of wood from the box beside the stove. Sliding it into the open flames, her hand slipped. Her wrist hit the side of the open circle. Her skin sizzled. Her wrist had a bad burn two inches wide and one inch long.

In the morning, Mary was preparing breakfast with a bandaged wrist. Bhikhu came in and stood beside her.

He asked, "What happened to your wrist?"

She showed her wrist to him.

He leaned close and quietly said, "Behind the illusions, dreams uncover the law. Time is our laboratory."

Now she had another gem of something to put into perspective. She wondered — *was he joking with me now?*

A car arrived on a sunny afternoon. A very neat looking, tall, slender, older man with white hair and a white cane got out of the car. He was blind but needed no assistance from the accompanying woman. He walked tall with confidence.

Mary greeted the couple. They walked and talked around the grassy area close to the main house.

"I've always been blind by day," the man was explaining. "At night I see everything clearly. I astral travel. I see colors of everything. I know where everything is and what it looks like. I've been here and had to come to put my feet on the ground here."

Mary felt validated to be able to talk about herself because here was a man who was extremely believable and he had no problem talking about himself. He was completely blind all his life, but could explain clearly and joyfully what he had been doing while astral traveling and what he had seen while out of body. He was only at the centre one afternoon, but left Mary with an admiration of a blind man who could see.

There was one woman, Edith, in the group that seemed to have taken Mary under her wing. She was a roly-poly older woman with white hair, who had lived in India for many years and was widowed when she met the Bhikhu. She had come from England, following the Bhikhu to Canada. For a few weeks, the Bhikhu had placed her in Mary's home in the city for Mary to help out until she got settled. Now, at the centre, Edith was interested in keeping her friendship with Mary.

It was a calm winter evening when Edith, Mary and a couple of other women decided to take a walk along the dirt road in the moonlight. They were marvelling at the millions of stars in the clear sky.

Edith stopped walking and instructed Mary, "Stop a minute and look at orgone energy in the air around you."

Mary stopped and looked into the night air for a few seconds.

"I can see it. Light. Dots of light ... I see millions of dots of light swirling and dancing in the air. A few moments ago, it seemed to be empty space that I could feel but not see. You've just shown me a way to see life in the fabric of the universe!"

The other women tried to see what Mary was seeing. After a few seconds, they simply walked on and did not comment.

Later, Edith and Mary sat in the kitchen to talk by the warm kitchen stove.

Edith told a story: "I was once consumed with jealousy, enough to consider killing someone. I was standing on a cliff. Below me were two important people in my life. One was a woman friend just a little younger than myself. The other was Bhikhu. They were just walking and talking on the beach below. I picked up the biggest rock I could manage with my two hands and held it over the cliff. I wanted to drop it on his head. Why him rather than her? If I killed him, she could not have his company. If I killed her, he would not be my friend. As I stood there holding the rock high in the air, I came to my senses and realized that killing is simply a moment of madness. I would instead have to deal with the war within me … my jealousy. We all have the instinct within us to defend our ideas, our bodies, our egos, our loved ones. We have the instinct to fight or take flight. What we do with those basic instincts makes the difference."

"Oh, I could never have the instinct to kill," Mary said and then stopped talking as she startled herself with a memory. There was silence as Mary realized where this conversation was now going. She resumed, "Actually, I did come to the point of having to make a decision of fight or flight. I had to leave my first husband because I knew I would have to fight, even to the death of one of us. He put my head through a wall and I still have a dent in my skull. I have a scar on my face. He pointed a gun at me. If I stayed as things were, I would have been dead or brain damaged. I could no longer allow him to beat me or threaten to beat the children. The children did get really scared at what they saw. My oldest son won't eat butter because he had climbed up onto the kitchen counter and got into butter when my husband came home and beat me right in front of him. My child witnessed it and my bloody face, so he won't eat butter ever since. I ran away with the children and even changed my name because I was so afraid of him and what he would do if he found me."

Edith said, "Yes, you made a decision on one of the basics of life."

Mary explained her dilemma. "I feel so sorry for him because he is just a tortured soul, a child of the world war. I carry guilt because he lost his children and I get word that he claims to still love me."

Edith asked, "What is love? Is love wanting to hurt and maybe destroy the person you love?"

"Of course not," Mary responded.

Edith continued, "The word 'love' is referred to in many ways with underlying meanings … the desire for possession … control … sex … romance. Possession means ownership. Control is a form of possession and exercising power. Sex is a basic animal instinct and can be had without love. Romance can be a mixture of fantasy, memory, and hero worship, and can be used to enhance a situation for sex, control, and possession. Romance has its own power and can lead to love. Love … pure love is unconditional. Love is without boundary. Love is intangible but when you love, you only want the best for the person you love. Love is infinite. When we have children, we learn how to love unconditionally. Love is so basic that animals love unconditionally. For example, we see that kind of unconditional love in dogs and horses. All animals love their offspring. We often get mixed up about what is love."

Mary was deep in thought and then responded, "I never really thought about it in this way. What about those people who seem to have love at first sight? I have met a guy who said he saw his wife walking. He only saw the back of her and knew he was seeing his wife. They are married now."

"Yes," Edith continued, "and the question arises — where was he before he was born? There was some memory of a relationship with his wife that comes from a life greater than his life on earth. It is not like he fell in love with her while meeting her and getting to know her. Instead, he knew her without even seeing her face. There was an invisible bond already in place that he recognized."

"It is so romantic." Mary was wistful.

"Yes, it is. I had better go to bed now."

Edith got up and disappeared out the door to find her bed in the new cabin built on the hill nearby.

Mary sat by the warm stove with a lot to think about. Once again, she felt validated, but also sad that as yet she had not known what it might be like to feel loved by an adult male. She craved love.

chapter six

Lessons

One afternoon Mary found a moment to just sit by the window under the staircase. She had managed to have the small record player hooked up to the only electrical light in the room. She laid the needle on her favorite record, Beethoven's Fifth Piano Concerto. 'The Emperor' filled the air around her as she sat looking out over the landscape and then she started to meditate. She let herself go to become one with the music. Years before coming here, Mary had experienced chakras opening while listening to this record. She was hoping after all this time, to recreate that experience.

As the music played low she felt the energy move in her body right down to her feet and up her body as the piano played higher sounds. She became a musical instrument with every sound vibrating within her. Up and down, around, down and up, softer and louder. In the middle range, the sound entered her heart, blossoming fully into a radiance of the most beautiful feeling she had ever experienced. It was all encompassing powerful. To stay with this blissful sensation forever would have been alright with her. Basking in it, she could feel her center radiating outward in beatific love. Her heart chakra had opened. The sound went lower and the energy from her heart moved down into the base of her spine. The heat was enormous, filling her lower body with a fire of sexual energy. Then it moved slightly forward and up into her belly, heating and blossoming there. As the music came out of the depths and rose, so did the energy. It rose and moved forward into another chakra at her navel, then smoothly back to her heart, blossoming fully in her chest. In her forehead, she could see inside her complete chest as clear as if a moving picture had been taken. A little flame of energy like a fire finger was moving up to her throat and wiggled around in there. It was still in her heart, but as though sending a feeler up to see if it could move up. Then it stopped. The finger of fire lowered back to her heart and all eventually cooled down.

Then, Mary experienced a throat so sore that she could barely talk.

In desperation, she hitched a ride with a guest to the city to ask the Bhikhu about her experience.

He listened patiently, seeming to be amused, and then asked her to wait in the living room while he disappeared for a few minutes.

He came back holding a steaming cup with pretty violets painted on it. She assumed the flowers on the cup meant he was friendly. He towered over Mary, holding the cup out toward her.

"Drink this."

She looked up at the towering man, feeling quite small. She gingerly took the hot cup and looked at the thick white broth with fear. "It's too hot!" she complained.

"Drink it."

"I can't. It's too hot!"

"Drink!" he commanded.

"I think I'm in the story of the three bears. It's too hot!"

He was clearly amused and then intent. "Drink it now!"

She sipped. "It's too hot!"

"More!"

She sipped again. "My mouth is burned."

"Kundalini can't get by your blocked throat chakra because your karma is in there. You have had a habit of building karma with words."

"But I don't say much."

Bhikhu just smiled and ended the session.

Back at the centre, her throat had healed quickly. There came the day when she put the record on again. This time, the Kundalini energy came alive again and moved up into her throat smoothly, flowing through and up into the third eye of her brow, blossoming there and moving to the top of her head, where at least a bud of the thousand petal lotus was felt. She knew her connection with a higher consciousness.

Later, she thought about it all. She knew what she felt and saw, but she also knew she was not any more enlightened than yesterday or last month. She thought her experiences with energy and explorations in the universe were simply antics like a mischievous child. She likened herself to the one light bulb connected to a larger source of energy that lit up intermittently, but the more she knew, the more she knew that she did not know the totality of the cosmos or God. And, furthermore, she was not going to pretend any more than that.

One of the men at the centre reported to the Bhikhu that Mary must be enlightened because of opening chakras. Mary had no knowledge of the telling until Bhikhu arrived.

Mary was ticked off at whoever reported such a thing, proving to herself that she was still very human.

Bhikhu asked her to go for a walk with him into the forest. He wanted alone time with her.

Someone had given him mukluks made by Inuit people for Christmas. They had no traction, so he was slipping and sliding on the snowy pathway. Mary gave him her arm to lean on as they made their way through the trees. Seeing comedy never stopped with her. She was amused because she was holding this giant man who towered over her and was her teacher, upright.

They talked briefly about chakras and what it all means. They both decided that Mary had not become enlightened over night and which they both thought was quite a joke, but she thought he seemed a bit disappointed.

While she had him alone, she complained, "I have no time to meditate. I get no help from James in anything. All he can think about is being out in the woods getting firewood. Then he comes back to the house and pretends to be a guru for the rest of the evening. He holds court with the men who now live here. The children are not getting any attention from him."

Mary paused, looking up to see if he was listening.

"I'm listening."

She went on, "When you give discourses, I am always in the kitchen preparing food or getting tea. I miss everything.

People sit around discussing the scriptures and I have no time. I feel like I'm being robbed of my intelligence. They all know more than I do."

She stopped to wave at the trees. "My complaints are bouncing off the trees and back into my ears. I don't even like the sound of myself."

Bhikhu responded, "There is no food value in feeding intellect with scriptures. You could spend your life studying scriptures and miss what you are meant to learn."

Mary continued, "As an example — those women ... you know who I mean ... stayed here all week. With Christmas over they came here for a holiday. They are housewives who have families. They are perfectly capable women. I worked my butt off for them all week while they meditated. Yesterday, I decided to have some time to myself. I played in the snow with my children. Then, I went to the other cabin to meditate for a few minutes. When I got back to the house, one of those women was on her high-horse because she had not had her afternoon tea served to her by me. She told me I had to make it. I told her to make it herself ... that I had just been meditating and she did not have to wait for me. She actually told me I have no right to meditate, that I am here to serve her. That makes me darnn mad."

"Self-destruction in the face of difficulties would be an error, would it not?"

"What do you mean?"

"Listen to yourself. Where is your balance? Why let those poor women destroy you? You are above that. You are capable of more. Do you think if someone told me that I have no right to meditate that I would take him seriously? Why would you?"

They walked for while in silence.

He broke the silence. "Sibelius is calmer. It's like these woods. You know, Sibelius was a hermit much of the time, hiding away by the sea to write. His music reflects his calm nature. Listen to it. You are like Beethoven, lots of ups and downs. Middle. Stay in the middle. A little more balance, not much swinging."

"You mean, flatten my emotions?"

"Yes."

"But, I like experiencing all the emotions. That's life."

"Life. You don't know life yet. You are too busy enjoying life here to get on with it. Don't spend so much time enjoying this earth."

"But, I like this earth. I love these trees. I get high on nature. I get high on music. I get high on color. Just look at all the colors in that tree trunk. It's not brown—it's multicolored. In all my life I've never gone low into depression! I don't even know what depression feels like. I just have indignation to happiness."

"You are in love with Maya … Illusions."

Bhikhu turned to walk toward the cabin, expecting Mary to follow. She watched to make sure he was staying upright.

She called after him. "I like it here!"

She thought to herself that she actually liked to debate with him over all the talk about life and death and a better life on other planes. On this day, she just wanted to be in the forest where she could feel the tranquility of trees and not worry about her soul and where it was going next, or whether or not she had become enlightened, and feeling foolish for ever mentioning her chakras to anyone.

The next time Bhikhu came to the centre, he brought a record of Sibelius along with Peter and the Wolf by Sergei Prokofiev for the children.

Mary listened to Sibelius, amused that to her ears, his music was as emotional as Beethoven.

While everyone was sleeping, Mary often worried about where the next food for the many would come from. Arranging the menus with inadequate contributions was a constant problem. This night she was going through her problems while tossing and turning, wondering—*whose shoulders does it fall on? Mine! And only mine! No one else has to deal with it! I try to keep up a good front for everyone and serve good meals. I have no food for breakfast. How can I face everyone with no food? How can I feed my own children? And there is James sleeping soundly with no worries. I can't share even a little problem with him.*

In the morning, Mary was putting wood in the stove and placing the kettle of water on top when she stopped and just stood there looking at the lion painted on the backsplash.

A few people were drifting in and talking to each other. Mary did not turn around. Bhikhu approached her and stood close by her side. His large presence felt comforting.

"What's wrong?" he asked quietly.

"Well, this time I really have no food to make breakfast with for this crowd. I can't pretend that everything is okay. I can't even make biscuits."

"What have we got?"

Mary shuffled around in the cupboard and brought out two onions. She went to the refrigerator and brought out four eggs. "That's it! Two onions and four eggs. That's all!"

"Good!"

Mary was surprised. "Good?"

Bhikhu smiled. "Good. Chop the onions into small pieces. Scramble the eggs over them. Cook them."

Bhikhu and Mary huddled together over the stove, cooking the eggs and onions.

Then Bhikhu instructed her to set the table.

She looked at him quizzically and then set the table as usual for a crowd of people.

More guests drifted in. Everyone took chairs expectantly. Mary guided her children into their places. The platter of eggs and onions started to be passed around. Bhikhu and Mary took two chairs nearest to the stove.

Mary's anxious eyes watched the platter go from one person to another. Bhikhu sat quietly. Each person took a helping and passed the serving platter on. Someone served the children and passed the platter on. The eggs and onions on the platter seemed to stay the same and never deplete. People all had a helping of food on their dishes and were happily eating and talking. The platter came back to Mary and Bhikhu with enough eggs and onions for their own breakfast. Bhikhu took the platter, served Mary and then himself.

Mary was amused. She whispered to Bhikhu, "The fish and loaves?"

He whispered back, "You see, you do not need to meditate as much as the others. Your service does you more good. Life is full of miracles. You do see!"

Mary thought for a moment and then whispered to him, "I had always known a security that did not come from material wealth. This experience has solidified knowing a richer source of well-being. I do see."

Life had more lessons. One snowy evening, Mary was wrapping a small block of cheese and hiding it in the farthest corner of a bottom shelf in the cupboard. It was safe because the cupboard was lined with tin and no mouse could get the cheese. And, no human could find it.

She was thinking—*all my life, my motto has been: God will provide. Now, after another weekend of feeding a crowd of city people, my cupboard is bare again. I have a small block of cheese and I keep hearing in my head that I must save it to feed my children.*

She was finishing cleaning the kitchen when there was a knock on the door. The two men who were Bhikhu's right hand men walked in and as they headed directly for the table, the first thing they said was, "Hi, Mary. Hey, we're hungry. Have you any cheese?"

Mary was stunned. Her mind ran fast with the reminder to save the cheese for the children.

The men sat at the table, smiling expectantly.

Cheese was dancing in Mary's mind—*am I being tested by some unseen source? How did these men know to ask for the very thing I hid? Not only that, but it would have taken the men just the amount of time to drive from the city to arrive at the meditation centre if they left the city at the time I hid the cheese.*

It was too weird and strange. She was thinking that she had to say no to having cheese and keep the cheese for the children. But, her honesty took hold. She decided she had to give what was asked for and that God would provide for her children.

Mary went to the cupboard and reached for the cheese.

She made a pot of tea and then watched the devouring of her children's only food.

"Thanks, Mary. We'll be off now." And they went out into the night. Mary listened to the car disappearing into the distance and wondered — *what the heck just happened?*

Mary spent a restless night and woke up to the answer. God did not provide that night.

Her oldest two children went to school with no lunch. She had given them the only money she had, which was a dime, to go to the store on lunch hour and buy a donut to share. Her children had gone hungry because she had misjudged. She felt awful.

She decided the lesson was obvious — her children were her responsibility — they were dependent on her — she had to look after her own children first, just as the Bhikhu had warned that first day — then, and only then could she look after the world — not the other way around.

It had snowed heavily all day. Bhikhu was in Scotland, so no guests were expected. The children were sleeping. James and one of the men living there and Mary were relaxing by the fire in the potbelly stove.

There was a knock on the kitchen door. Mary opened the door to a snow covered man.

"I'm stuck on the road. I'm trying to get to my cabin by the lake."

"Come in," Mary greeted.

She helped the man out of his snow covered outer wear and invited him to have tea.

As the evening went on and there was nothing needing to be done, Mary brought out a deck of cards. She had learned a long time ago, how to read cards and offered to play around with the guys just for fun.

As she read the cards for the guest, he seemed intensely interested. She had no idea if any of what she was saying was making sense to him.

It had stopped snowing. He wanted to go, but needed the guys to help dig him out of the snow. They all dressed and went out. Mary had a few minutes to enjoy herself, by herself in the warmth of the fire.

The next morning, brilliant sunshine was streaming in through the kitchen window as Mary put wood into the stove for cooking breakfast.

James and his companion man came in and stood by the table.

"Breakfast not ready?" James asked.

Mary turned to face them. "You guys need to examine your heads. You are useless to me. You bring in wood but I am on my own for absolutely everything else. Even in winter all you guys think about is yourselves. You treat me like I'm your servant. You ..."

Mary was interrupted by a knock on the kitchen door. James answered. The man who had arrived unexpectedly the night before stood there with a large bottle in his raised hand.

"Hi, I have a something for Mary."

James reached for it. The man bypassed James and walked straight into the kitchen in his snowy boots to Mary and handed the bottle to Mary.

"This is thanks for the wonderful reading last night. You helped me."

"How did I help?"

"Just know you helped."

He turned and went out the door, closing the door behind him, leaving James with his mouth open.

Mary read the label on the bottle while the men strained their necks to read the label. The label read: TEACHER'S WHISKEY made in SCOTLAND.

The men burst out laughing.

"Why is this funny?" Mary asked.

James laughed, "You have to drink this!"

He took the bottle from her hands and opened it. He poured whisky into three cups and handed one to Mary.

She put the cup to her mouth to taste. She cringed.

Both men laughed loudly.

James could hardly contain himself with laughter, "Payback. Bitter as your words."

Mary responded, "It's rare that I express anger to you. You're getting off easy."

Mary never knew what happened to the rest of the whisky. It just disappeared. She was never to know what the man was so grateful for. But, the big question was how it happened that an unseen power made a stranger go to the store and buy such a gift that was for a non-drinking woman. Mary wondered how on earth was it that this man was the bearer of such a gift to her of Teacher's Whiskey made in Scotland while the teacher was actually in Scotland. She felt that it was a reminder from a long way across the ocean that distance and separation had no bearing in a connection that overcomes distance and time — and somehow there is an all-knowing across all space and time. While the men consumed whiskey, Mary had thoughts to consume.

James was not finished with punishment for Mary's criticism.

Mary had made a small sculpture of clay. It kind of looked like herself with a child on her lap. It was greenware because she had no kiln to fire it. She had set it in the middle of the round coffee table by the doorway in the large room just off the kitchen. She came into the room to see the sculpture laying on the table, smashed. Her eyes followed across the room where James and his buddy were seated facing the doorway as though in a theatre, waiting for her to react.

Mary deliberately ignored the sculpture and did not show any reaction. She was aware that the guys were disappointed.

She sat beside the stove and pretended nothing was bothering her.

James started rubbing his chin and as usual, started his evening of waving his hands and talking as though he was the teacher to all in the room.

Mary closed her eyes to relax and meditate, ignoring James.

Suddenly, she felt like she was falling backward. She struggled to stay upright even though her physical body was upright. She felt herself getting larger and larger. She felt like she was immense—a giant. She opened her eyes to check herself out. Her body was sitting perfectly straight in her chair and she was very conscious. She looked around to see how large her body had become. Her body seemed to be the same size as the others in the room. She realized it was her astral body that was so large the she felt immense power. She could feel it building, expanding even more. Time stood still. She had found the timeless zone. She could see the people and the world around were all in 'Time', but she was in a timeless place. She held her hands in the air and moved them slowly back and forth. Her hands were in front of her in all positions at all times. There was all time and no time. Everything happened at once.

Mary had the fleeting thought about how small James was regardless of his big ego. Simultaneously, James grabbed his head and begged, "Don't think of me! My head! Don't! It hurts my head."

Mary was surprised and looked at James.

He yelled, "Stop. Don't think about me."

Mary rushed out of the room, not knowing what to do. She stood beside her cooking stove, about as far away as she could get from James and looked back at the wall between the rooms. From there she could see right through the wall and see the men. James was holding his head and his buddy just looked plain scared.

James was desperate, "Don't think about me," he yelled.

Mary turned her back to them, thinking this was all too strange, and wondered what James was thinking.

James hollered, "No! Leave my head alone. Don't think of me!"

Mary's body jolted in surprise. It was over. She was left with her wondrous thoughts—*it really happened*—*he knew when I was thinking of him.* The knowledge of her greater self and what happened would stay with her for a while.

James asked Mary to cut his hair. As she was doing so, he announced that he would go to the city to find work.

He had not discussed his plan with her, so it was a surprise. "When you find work, then what?" she asked.

"I'll work a few days a week and be here on weekends."

"What about us all moving back to the city?"

"Maybe. I'll find work and then we'll decide."

Later that day, James stood at the door in his red plaid jacket and in his hand was a suitcase. He turned back to simply say, "Bye." and left with no physical contact.

It was his red plaid jacket in the open doorway that twigged a kind of knowing for Mary. It was as though she had seen this scene before somewhere, somehow, even though it was happening only now. Suddenly, she had a gut realization that he was never coming back to live with her. This was his farewell.

Mary now knew what had bothered her that very first day on the meditation centre—that horrible, foreboding feeling was a glimpse of what was happening now. James was leaving and would not return when Mary was feeling most vulnerable. She was in the very early stage of pregnancy.

A few nights ago, she was aware of a small, blue, ethereal ball floating around the bedroom. It came closer and closer, until it merged with Mary. She knew then that she had become pregnant with a soul that needed or wanted to be born to her. Mary had not heard of blue balls, but she knew instinctively what it meant.

Bhikhu sent a monk who wore only saffron robes. He was to be a presence at the centre while Mary and the children were living alone in the middle of winter, and at least he was to make sure she had wood for fires. He lived in the other cabin but spent most of his time in the main cabin with the family. He was teaching the children a little bit of Sanskrit and trying to play with the children. He kept the wood and water coming.

The evening was calm with the children in their beds. Mary and the monk were relaxing by the potbellied stove. Mary was so relaxed that she nodded off while in her chair. Being pregnant, it was easy to fall asleep—**Mary found herself in the room where James was in a sexual encounter with a woman who Mary thought was her friend. Mary was standing right in the room with them.**

Mary woke up with a start. The monk was in his chair, watching over her.

Realizing she was being watched, Mary pretended nothing happened. She said nothing about astral traveling while sleeping and actually witnessing James and her friend.

Mary needed to go to the city to find James and get a straight story and figure out what to do for her future.

James chose to meet in a restaurant. The waiter was taking the order. James asked for beef steak for both of them.

"Steak?" Mary asked, "We've been vegetarians for two years."

"Steak!" James insisted.

The waiter walked away. This was Mary's moment to say, "You had sex with my friend."

"How do you know?"

"I was there."

"What do you mean you were there?"

"Not deliberately. I was in the room. By astral travel, I guess. I would not want to do that on purpose. Why, James?"

"She was just like an old shoe. Fit well but not exciting."

"Why? Why if like an old shoe? Why at all?"

"Some things are out of my control."

"I'm pregnant."

"But you were not pregnant when I left."

"You've only been gone a few of weeks. Of course, I was pregnant."

James' eyes got hard. "It must be someone else's."

"You know I never sleep around."

"That's been your problem! You are behind everyone else spiritually because you haven't been sleeping around."

"You really believe that?"

"I'm serious. Grow up. Sleep around."

"But what about the children, the coming baby?"

"Get an abortion! It's not mine."

The waiter planted two steaks onto the table.

James continued, "I'm staying in the city. You can live at the meditation centre."

"You mean you are leaving me?"

"Yes, if you want to call it that."

Mary responded, "This poor cow died just to be thrown in the garbage."

Mary's next stop was to have a talk with Bhikhu. He was seated with the window behind him. His face was in shadow with light coming over his shoulders. His eyes were darkly sympathetic. He dropped a deck of Tarot cards at Mary's feet.

"You are experiencing the dark night of the soul."

Mary stared at the cards. The nine of swords and ten of swords lay exposed.

Bhikhu continued, "Ahh, but don't let that be all. There is also end to delusion. You cannot stay there. You must experience darkness to know light. The dark night of the soul does not last forever."

Mary asked, "Will James come back to me?"

"I don't know. Your life does not depend on James."

"But, the children!"

"Your children's lives do not depend on him."

"He should not be allowed to run off and be irresponsible. What sort of teaching is this?"

"I came to teach sinners. It would do you no good for me to order him returned."

"But I'm pregnant."

"Then you have much to live for."

"I love him."

There was silence while Mary thought about how she had just lied.

Then Bhikhu continued, "Love! You call that love! Possessive attachment! You love your children in the most selfless love you know. Love is not selfish, not rooted in your own desires."

"And James, does he know love?"

"James! James will keep you from knowing love. James will tie up your energy. He will use you. Go! You only think you are unhappy. This is your illusion and delusion. You may not believe me, but there is someone else for you in the future. You will continue to live for many years in a balanced way. It is not time for you to become a renunciant. You must experience earthly life in abundance, but with a greater understanding than the average person."

Through the log cabin window, a giant fire caught her eye. Mary saw that the monk was outside wearing his saffron robes and big winter boots. He had built a giant bonfire that was several feet in diameter and at least ten feet high in the middle of a field of white snow.

Mary came out of the house and stood beside him to gaze at the fire with curiosity. Sparks of fire flew high against a black sky sprinkled with millions of twinkling stars. It was a wondrous scene.

He explained, "This is a cleansing fire. I've thrown in more of the old mink cages. Anything you want to throw in the fire?"

"Maybe … I think so."

She ran back to the house and up the staircase with her boots on. Oddly, her children were continuing to sleep as she grabbed an armful of her clothing without inspecting anything. Before leaving, she paused and grabbed a paper box.

She ran down the staircase.

At the bonfire, she threw the armful of clothing into the fire, somehow feeling she was throwing her broken relationships away. Then she opened the box and threw sheets of manuscript into the fire along with all the research notes.

With cold snow under her feet and the heat of fire on her face she watched writing on papers catch flames that slowly shrunk the papers and curled them into charcoal, releasing into smoke all the ideas and hard work of months.

She stood there wondering—*should I consider this my failure or perhaps a waste of time?—all those hours in the library doing research and the evenings writing the manuscript?*

As her clothing burned before her eyes, she saw the mauve dress her mother had sewn for her years ago, and a broach of three intertwined rings that her mother had given to her just before she got on the train to come back to the meditation centre. The broach had been attached to an item landing in the fire and now she could not retrieve it. Her mother's smiling face loomed before her and the sound her mother's sewing machine mingled with the sound of the fire.

As Mary walked away from the fire, she was not sure she had gotten rid of past relationships in a fire ceremony. She only knew that she had thrown away all her clothes and had practically nothing to wear for starting her life over again. She mourned the loss of things her mother had given her.

In the middle of the night, Mary woke up and gazed around the room at the log walls. She had been dreaming: **she and the children were in a van driving the country road alongside the meditation centre acreage. The road suddenly had a large crevice across it that looked like an** earthquake had split it. It was so wide and deep that it was impossible to cross.

Mary knew the dream meant her stay at the centre was over.

Bhikhu insisted that James arrange an apartment in the city and pay the rent for it. James was also told he must provide food. James complied with a barest minimum of support causing some people to tell him outright that he must do better.

Mary knew James' support would be until he could justify not doing it. After one visit with the four year old daughter, he refused to see any of the children for any time in present or future.

Then, he was off to Mexico.

Mary took brief walks in the evenings up and down the block she now lived on. The lights behind the windows meant to her that people had security of family, marriage and a secure home. She craved all of that, but especially she wanted a home for her children. It seemed to her that she was constantly pregnant and homeless. It was an exaggerated time of loneliness. She spent countless hours just sitting and staring at a blank wall, and wondering what to do next.

James was back and surprised Mary by inviting her to a house party. She sewed herself a sexy but suitable dress for the occasion. He picked her up and drove her to the house, then abandoned her inside the doorway. There she stood, six months pregnant with a big belly and alone when she discovered a sixteen year old girl was waiting for James.

The happy, seemingly innocent teenager was flaunted in Mary's face, in front of everyone.

After the months of James' mind games, Mary had enough. He was not seeing the children at all, so any future plans need not include him at all.

Six and a half months pregnant now, she wanted to get as far away from James as possible. She needed to take control of her own life and hopefully give the children a decent life without controversy. A photographer friend had expressed interest in Mary's negative retouching machine which had been her source of income and the only thing she owned worth any money. Selling it got just enough money to board a train with her children, and hopefully have a month's rent and a little food for starting over.

chapter seven

Starting Over

Mary and her four children boarded a train heading west. This would be the second time Mary and the kids left everything they owned behind. Again, all they were bringing were clothing and a few pillows and blankets. Mary packed all the children's toys but they would disappear along the way. The family was headed across the country to—not knowing what. She did not know what they would find, except it was four days to the end of the earth, the farthest distance from James that she could get to.

It had to be a place where she and her children could live with nature on very little money. It had to be by the ocean and hopefully they could live close enough to a beach to be able to walk there. She was looking to the future with nothing but simple hope.

A handsome, middle-aged conductor had helped the family put their boxes and baby stroller into the baggage car and board the train. He seemed to be especially interested in what was going on.

On the small money Mary had to buy the train trip, she had booked only one bunk for sleeping and meal tickets for half the meals the family really needed. Her plan was that they would trade around over the whole trip and be okay.

Mary was sitting up in the day car while she had bedded the children in the sleeping car. The conductor approached her and offered his private sleeping room to her. Mary was tired, but she needed to be up and available to her children. More than that she was afraid of the conductor's intentions. She had no way of knowing what they were.

"Thanks, but I'm okay."

"You have only one bunk and you're traveling for four days. You have only limited food vouchers. I can help you. My quarters can be yours."

"Really, I'm fine. The kids and I will alternate for the dining room. We'll alternate sleeping arrangements."

The conductor looked disappointed and walked away.

The next night, Mary was tired. She and the kids piled into the one bunk. It was an upper bunk assigned to her, so it was awkward for all to get comfortable. Just as they were all sleeping, the conductor knocked on the bunk.

"You can't all be in the bed," he demanded. "Someone has to get out."

Mary got out with the smallest child as the conductor stood by watching.

"You can sleep in my private quarters," he again offered.

"Thank you. I'll be fine."

Sitting upright with her baby on her lap, Mary wondered about the conductor's offer—was it out of sympathy for a pregnant woman? She had no way of knowing. As the train chugged on through the night, Mary wondered how this trip would end. Earth was not solid in a fast moving train. The only thing she knew was that she had great hope of arriving at the Pacific Ocean with all her children and starting a new life where her children could be happy and safe.

By day, the older children wanted to explore the car with an upper deck of windows.

"Sure," Mary agreed. "Just don't get lost. Come right back here."

While the children were gone, a strange woman and man approached Mary. They stood in the aisle towering over her.

"Hello. My name is Carol and this is my husband Stone. We have been talking with your children in the viewing car. We run a school in the United States and we would like to have your children in our school."

"My children are staying with me." Mary was apprehensive that this couple might be dangerous.

Stone said, "We're offering our school free to you. It won't cost you anything."

"As I said, my children are not available. My children stay with me in Canada. Please do not talk to them about this. They are not going anywhere."

Mary was now scared for the safety of her children.

When the children returned, Mary instructed, "From now on I need you all to stay close to me so that I can see you at all times. If you can't see me, I can't see you. I'll go with you next time to the viewing car."

Arriving four days later at the west coast, Mary and the children found themselves in a grand, marble train station. It felt cold, opulent, exciting, impressive all at once. She had never seen such a magnificent building and this was the first footsteps into the start of the new life she wanted.

Her great relief was that all her children were still safe with her and that no one got lost along the way. There was no sign of the couple who she had been afraid would maybe kidnap a child.

Mary placed the children to sit on a long, brown, shiny bench where she could watch them while she made calls on a payphone at a desk nearby. She called newspaper ads. Dozens of phone calls later, renting a place to live in with four children was disappointing. No one wanted children.

Then she called social services and the YWCA. All services questioned her about what money she had. She admitted to everyone that she had enough money for a month's rent. Each one told her to rent an apartment because so long as she had any money at all, she was on her own. There was no help available to her family even when she explained that no landlords wanted children.

There was a hotel across the street. Out of desperation, Mary needed to use some of her money to rent a room. In that tiny room, they all slept in a crowded bed and ate garlic sausage, cheese and bread picnic style on a blanket on the floor for the next couple of days. Mary continued the phone calls in the hotel lobby and got turned down every time.

On the third day a man on the phone said, "Yes, I have an apartment for you. Come to my house."

Mary packed up the children and tried to sign out of the hotel room. She was half an hour past the signing out time.

The woman behind the desk demanded Mary pay for a whole next day rental of the room. Mary tried to explain that she was only a half hour late. The woman could clearly see that Mary was pregnant with four little kids, but she insisted. Mary paid. Her money was dwindling fast.

It was a hot summer day of clear sky and sunshine. Mary had left all their luggage at the train station in baggage, but did have the stroller for her baby. She and her four children started walking. They walked to the long, high bridge and crossed it. She was lost, not knowing the city. She turned the family around and walked back over the bridge.

At the end of the bridge, she yelled down to someone working below that she needed to get to a certain address and was lost. The man below instructed her to cross the bridge and go a few more blocks up the hill to the address.

Walking the bridge for the third time, Mary felt something snap in her lower body. It alarmed her for a second, but she needed to ignore it and find the man who by now was sounding like her guardian angel.

At the house, Mary was relieved immediately when she saw that the man was surrounded by his small children and a wife. She felt safe. He accepted her and her children without asking for references. He was happy to help. He drove the family back to the train station in his big car and picked up their belongings. He then took the family to a two bedroom unfurnished apartment, which was the upper floor of a house that he managed.

Mary was to find out that this man filled his rental properties as much as possible with women needing help and in turn he asked for nothing but the payment of rent.

Mary was to be grateful to him for the rest of her life and would think of him as a guardian angel because he placed her and her children in a home just in time …

That night, Mary and the children were sleeping on the hard linoleum floor with only blankets and pillows. She tossed and turned all night long with mild contractions. She hoped that they were only false labor.

She had promised the children that if they found an apartment, they would go to the beach the next day. So, in the morning, Mary walked a couple of blocks to the nearest grocery store for a picnic lunch. Then, she and the children found the bus stop back where the grocery store was and headed across the city to the beach where Mary wanted to eventually live close to because a woman on the train had said, "That's the place to live."

At the beach, the children were happy, exploring the sand and nearby water's edge. Mary had already done a fair amount of walking that morning, so she was glad to just sit and relax in the shade under a large willow tree with her baby and just take in her new surroundings.

She had bravely brought her children thousands of miles across the country and now as the day wore on, she realized that she was afraid of taking another step on the beach. She was rooted to the ground in the shade under the tree, from where she watched her children play. She felt the tree was guarding her. She looked up at the trunk of the tree just above her and it actually had what looked like a friendly face in the bark. She had kept her promise to the children even though she had labor pains all night long.

It was turning out not to be false labor. All day the pains had not subsided, instead they had been getting more intense.

In the evening, the children came to tell her that there was a showboat show happening on the stage, "… just over there!"

Mary looked over to where they were pointing. It was not far, but she could not go. As the sun was setting about 9 p.m. She was in excruciating painful labor that she could no longer deny. She needed to get the children back to the apartment.

They found the bus stop and waited as the sun was beginning to set across the water and sand that they could still see. Mary was trying to keep her labor pains to herself. She worried because it was going to be difficult—they were going to have to transfer to a second bus to get home and she had a one year old baby and stroller to carry in and out of buses.

The bus ride seemed to take forever. She was alarmed at having a hard time sitting still, but trying to keep a calm exterior. She was afraid of giving birth right on the bus or on the street somewhere.

As they made their way across the city, Mary was worried about how to make sure her children were safe and taken care of so that she could go to the hospital. The only solution she could think of was to call social services for help. That scared her because in those days children were being apprehended for this very reason, or any reason when women were without husbands. She was in a turmoil of fear of losing her children while the physical labor pains were getting worse and she was trying to hold her body together in silence.

As Mary and the children entered the hallway of the house, they immediately were greeted by the young married couple living in the main floor suite. The woman was visibly pregnant. The couple had been waiting, simply intending to introduce themselves.

Mary explained that she needed to use their telephone quickly because she was in labor and had to arrange care for the children, and then she needed to have a taxi to get to the hospital right away because her baby was premature.

The couple immediately offered to look after the children. A pregnant woman and her longshoreman husband took Mary from excruciating fear to knowing the world was a good place. She could go and give birth knowing her children were safe. Mary was convinced this was the second encounter in two days with guardian angels. She felt extremely lucky and well taken care of by some unseen power.

The doctor was saying, "You got here just in time. Why are you covered in sand?"

Mary was amused regardless of her predicament. She was thinking—*here I am, giving birth to a premature baby and the doctor wants to know why I am covered in sand.*

Amazingly, she had somehow, by some miracle, gotten there in time. She gave birth within minutes to a girl only two and a half pounds at two and a half months early. She only had a glimpse of her tiny baby before they whisked her away to intensive care.

The next day, Mary was escorted to look at her baby through a window. She was not allowed to go near her. The baby lay in an incubator with tubes running here and there.

The paediatrician stood beside her and explained, "Your baby only has a fifty percent chance of living. We will do everything possible to help her. But it will be a miracle if she survives and has a healthy life."

As Mary was looking at her baby's hands, she could see powerful energy in the tiny hands. It was as though Mary could see that this baby wanted to live and be healthy.

"I believe in miracles," she said softly.

She named her baby Faith at that moment.

Mary thought it ironic that just to prove who her father was, as a newborn the baby looked like James.

Mary had been placed in an unwed mothers' ward because when she was admitted to the hospital, she had admitted that she was separated from her husband. The ward had other single women of all ages in the two rows of beds. They were about to give birth or had given birth. The woman in the bed beside Mary was knitting a coat for herself as though she had no care in the world because she was giving her baby up for adoption, and she was just waiting to be released from the hospital.

Mary found out that all the women, young and older, were giving their babies up for adoption. Mary was dumbfounded.

In the middle of her third night in the hospital, she was woken up by a male doctor accompanied by another man standing beside her bed. They were both dressed in white.

The doctor said, "You have a uterine infection that must be treated right away."

They went away.

In the morning, Mary asked a nurse about the treatment for the infection.

The nurse asked, "What infection?"

"Two doctors came in the night to tell me I have an infection. When does the treatment start?"

"What doctors? What infection?"

The nurse looked at the chart attached to the bottom of the bed. "According to your chart, you have no infection and no doctor visited you last night."

Mary's grandmother, who died of a staph infection on the third day after giving birth to her fifth child, had been on Mary's mind off and on thoughout the pregnancy. The doctors had woken Mary up on the third night after she had given birth to her fifth child. Mary was wondering how come it was so real that she could remember what the doctor looked like. Somehow, a recreation of her grandmother's third day had just happened and then it did not happen.

The next drama was a social worker visiting. She was a large woman with a veneer of a marching soldier towering over Mary in her bed.

"I've come to help you give your baby up for adoption."

Mary was shocked. "My baby is not available for adoption."

"You don't need another baby. Adoption…"

Mary interrupted forcefully, "My baby is not available for adoption. Please leave."

"Think it over. I'll be back."

The woman left but returned the following day, and the following day, and the day afterward to tower over Mary.

"Hello. You've had chance to think about adoption…"

Mary was increasingly angry. "Go away! You've been here every day for a week. You know my answer. My baby is coming home with me when she weighs five pounds. Stay away from her!"

The woman continued her argument, "Mary, you don't need another child. You already have four and no husband."

"Having no husband is no reason to take a child. My baby is not available for adoption. Go away!"

Mary left the hospital but her baby had to stay, still too small to come home. It worried Mary that her baby was behind locked doors. She had not once been able to touch her baby and there was a lurking social worker. Mary had no choice but to leave without her baby.

She had no money, so she walked home. It was a long way. Almost home, Mary was crossing the street in a crosswalk, unable to move faster when a city bus driver was driving fast and stopped suddenly to yell, "Hey, lady. Move it!"

Mary looked up at his angry face with an angry gaping mouth. She did not answer. She wondered—*how would he handle walking my miles in my sandals?* She had been feeling brave for many days through a long journey, but that bus driver made her realize how vulnerable she was really feeling in a society of kindness and hostility. She felt like crying, but would not. She just needed to continue her journey and get home to be with her children.

Home finally. Her children were around her. The rooms were bare without even one piece of furniture but she was home with her children.

Within a few minutes, her ten year old son had a meltdown. They were standing in their bare living room by the windows.

He was crying, "I feel like jumping out the window!"

Mary was shook up. She had not expected this. "I'm sorry I've disappeared for a week. I couldn't help it."

Mary put her arms around him. "We have a new baby but she is too small to bring home. We have to wait until she's bigger. We'll be okay from now on. I won't be leaving again."

Her son stopped crying and seemed to be comforted. He went to join the other children in the other room.

Mary stood alone at the window feeling like she betrayed her son. She had no idea of how they were going to be okay from this day forward. She felt devastated.

As she stood there looking out at the mountains in the distance, she wondered how to give her son and all her children a better life than she had done so far. Through everything, this was the first time she imagined giving her children up to some family on a ranch somewhere where they could be happy living in the country with stable parents — a life she had never been able to give her children.

Her heart ached as she hit an emotional bottom like never before. At that moment, somehow words were impressed on her, *"You can have it any way you want."*

Mary heard the words clearly and realized that if she could have it any way she wanted, then she could sink or swim. She would choose to swim.

At that moment Mary felt that she could make a good life with her children. She had just had a once in a lifetime experience with despair, but as an eternal optimist, Mary chose tomorrow to be better.

Mary had no money left, not even enough to buy a loaf of bread, and no support. Her only choice was to go to work. She had four small children and a premature baby who would need special care when she came home. A babysitter would not do under the special circumstances. She did the unthinkable. She applied for temporary social assistance while realizing that she may be in for a fight.

A social worker came to visit. She tried to convince Mary that with her working background, she had all the necessary experience to land a job right away. Mary refused, explaining her reasons. After an hour of back and forth, she was given the financial assistance needed. Mary was relieved that she lived in Canada and had a chance to start over like this. She also was grateful that she would never have to beg the fathers of her children for support. At least in that part of her life, she could keep her pride.

From then on, Mary and the children got on with enjoying each other and starting over. With the bedding rolled up on the floor, and a kitchen table made of cardboard boxes, they went shopping for oil paints and canvases.

Her ten year old son painted the mountain ranges as he saw them on the journey. Her eight year old son painted a portrait of his mother. They were having fun.

There was a knock on the door. The social worker from the hospital was standing on the staircase one step below Mary. Now Mary was at eye level with her. The social worker had a handful of papers and waved them as she talked.

"I have your adoption papers here. All I need is your signature."

Mary felt extremely determined. "No! My baby is not available for adoption. If you do not leave us alone, I will throw you down the stairs."

The social worker was stunned. After a pause, she turned and retreated fast down the staircase. She never returned.

Mary was left with the surprise that all she saw was the woman's back as she ran away. Mary wondered if there was going to be a retaliation about her threat, but there was none. Mary wondered if she could have carried out her threat. She was sure that as a mother losing her child, she could be provoked into an unexpected reaction. She thought about how animals will protect their babies and go crazy with grief when their young are ripped away. Mary realized that she had the basic instinct of an animal protecting her babies. Mary's baby was behind locked doors and she had no access. Regardless of her aversion to violence, and regardless of the teachings she had just been through with Bhikhu, she was going to defend her motherly right and confront the aggressor. Fight or Flight? Mary had only one choice. She was not about to be passive. It was quite a thought that if the woman had not run away, what might have happened.

The day arrived when Mary's baby was five pounds and she came home. There were a brief few days when the world seemed cozy and right. All of her children were together and safe. No one was bothering the family. Her baby only had a cardboard box with a pillow as a bed, but Mary was happy — *cardboard table, cardboard cradle, bare floors, who cares, we are healthy and together, and starting our new life.*

Mary's daughter, the middle child was about to have a fifth birthday. She was unrelenting in a wish that her 'dad' should come for her birthday. Mary had to accept that her daughter only knew James as a father.

One hot day, Mary and her children, and a woman who lived in the basement suite with her two kids, went to a beach at the foot of a row of houses. While there, Mary made a wish that she wrote on the seawall just by picking up a piece of charcoal and writing with it. She simply wrote: *James come for birthday.*

Mary was not finished wishing to please her daughter. That night she laid on the floor in her blanket. Beside her, she had a lit birthday candle. It was only a tiny birthday cake candle because that's all she had in anticipation of the birthday. It would burn out quickly, so she made a quick prayer to the candle for James to come for her daughter's birthday.

Mary really believed James would never come and all this wishing was in vain because he had never cared about the children, and why would he travel the thousands of miles for them now. She had not communicated with him directly to inform him of anything, nor to ask for anything.

As the candle burned out, Mary fell asleep. She was woken by a voice saying, "He will come."

She was startled and fully awake, looking around. The voice had been real and very clear, but there was no one around.

There was a knock on her door. She opened it. James and a woman stood on the staircase. As though nothing was out of the ordinary, James expected to be welcomed along with a girlfriend — And, he was.

Though extremely surprised, Mary was glad that her daughter's wish had come true even if he thought it okay to bring a girlfriend. More than that, Mary was amazed that the words she heard in the middle of the night had proclaimed a truth. She would never tell anyone because it was too unbelievable.

When James told Mary where they were living while in town, she was wonderstruck because where she had written her wish on the seawall was directly below the house where he was staying. The house was only about half a block away and looked out onto that very beach.

Mary had little emotional reaction to James, so being kind and welcoming to his girlfriend was not a problem. The birthday was a success.

James and his girlfriend stayed around longer than expected, although once again, after the birthday he ignored the children. He was in town, but nowhere to be seen.

Mary's oldest boy was suddenly not wanting to go to school. He seemed ill, so she took him to see a doctor. The doctor referred the boy to the hospital for neurological testing. He had electrodes placed around his head for some testing, then he and his mother were sent to a room for an interview. What Mary did not realize, is that behind a mirror, the interview was being monitored by other medical staff, none of which had been or would be introduced to her. Her son was asked about his life at home and at school. He expounded excitedly about oil painting pictures with his mom.

At the end of the interview, a consultation was held behind closed doors. Then the neurologist came back to exclaim, "Your son needs to be taken out of his present school and away from his teacher. That's where his troubles are. Your home life is absolutely fine. Move your child away from that school and his health will return."

After all the troubles they had come through, that was the last thing Mary expected to hear. Then the neurologist told Mary how other doctors had monitored the interview from behind the mirror and the consensus was that she was providing what her son needed.

Mary looked at the grey glass, wanting to see who was behind it and saw nothing.

As if luck was on her side, Mary immediately found an old house within walking distance to the beach where she had almost given birth. It had been her wish to live close to that beach since a woman on the train had told her that was the place to live.

The family moved into the house. Mary and the children started the life she had wanted. She found a large Persian rug at the Salvation Army outlet and the salesman gave it to her with an under mat for three dollars, and he had it delivered for her. She made large cushions to sit on around the Persian rug in the living room. She bought two guitars for ten dollars each at a corner store. She gave one to her sons and kept one for herself to play. Baby Faith was a miracle—healthy, happy and developing normally. Mary enrolled her five year old daughter in ballet lessons. Her sons were happily following their interests of science and music. Without actual furniture, she had created a really nice home that the family was happy in, and they walked to the beach any time they wanted. They had nature at their doorstep just as she had wanted, and it cost no money to experience the wild ocean and all it offered in fresh air and a sense of freedom. It was exactly like she had wished for—a dream come true and the family had been protected from lurking dangers at every step along the journey.

Their new home was in a neighborhood where there was no judgment about a woman being a single parent. There was no judgment about what her sex life might have been. Mary felt free, no longer having to hide that she was a single parent.

It was one afternoon while on the beach that Mary realized she had found herself. She realized she had been identifying herself with the men in her life. As she looked out at the ocean, she thought—*I am ME with children!*

With her boys in school and the small children playing in the sand around her, Mary laid in the sand, sifting sand that glistened differing colors in the sunshine through her fingers. She was completely relaxed, contemplating the universe in grains of sand — her world was beautiful and right. She was thinking that somehow she had come to completeness within herself and was simply marvelling at grains of sand.

During this time, Mary discovered her brother had also arrived in the same city after a marriage break-up. He also was starting over. Now she had more family than her children.

Instead of going back to where he came from, James sold a car to Mary's brother because he wanted to go to India. It turned out that James had only borrowed the car from someone else at the meditation centre and drove it across the country. James took off to India with Mary's brother's money, leaving his girlfriend Louise behind — jilted in a strange city.

Louise glommed onto Mary. Even though she continued to live in a different apartment, she took refuge in Mary's home every day as though she was one of the family.

Mary had just come from the meditation centre where her life was looking after all sorts of people. Here she was, looking after James' girlfriend. It was as though Mary had another child. The irony was not lost on her, but Mary had an open heart. She had healed from the trauma of James. It had been a short three years and two babies, but she was over James. She could look after the insecure woman he had jilted.

The problem was that Louise had jealousy. Mary could see the tentacles in Louise's eyes and know that another of her clothing would go missing. It seemed that Louise was trying to become Mary and get as close as possible by taking everything she could to identify herself as Mary. Whatever Mary was wearing, Louise would take a fancy to and steal it. Mary would meet Louise on the street where she would wear Mary's clothes to go shopping.

Mary thought that Louise was so insecure with a hole that she tried to fill with things. She thought Louise admired her and was jealous at the same time. Somehow, Mary never had the heart to confront Louise about her clothing, she just let it happen.

Soon Louise had another boyfriend, but just as soon as they got together, he was sent to jail for possession of marijuana. Louise was alone again, pregnant and dependent on Mary.

Louise was present when a letter arrived from James. He was stranded in India with no money. He was asking for Mary to send money to him. He offered a promise that if she would send money, he would come back to Mary, and when he got back, he would take her oldest son on a motorcycle trip to Mexico.

Louise said, "Good."

Mary looked at her with surprise, "Good? I'm not sending money. I don't want him back. I will never let my son go with him on a motorcycle to Mexico."

Louise said, "But, he's stranded. He needs money to come back."

"I don't care if he is stranded. He can find his own way."

Louise continued to argue, "I think you should take him back."

Mary let loose finally, "Never! I did send him ten dollars a few weeks ago when he said he was starving and that came out of food money for feeding my children. I regret sending it. How many times can I be that foolish? I'm not paying his way back. I have children to care for. He has never, and I mean never, helped to support the children. I am completely on my own to look after five children. No! I don't care if he never gets back."

After a moment of letting Louise digest that, Mary continued, "Look, I need to explain something to you. James and I will never be together again. It seems to me that we came together to be explorers. We did that. We found the Bhikhu and the teachings, and from there we parted. I have two beautiful children that are my gifts from my relationship with him. I have no regrets. I have no hard feelings. But, I need to get on with my life."

One afternoon, two men from the coffee house days arrived. They were men who tried to convince Mary that it was all the women's fault and certainly no fault to men. Mary was completely taken by surprise to see them at her door since she thought she was well rid of them. But, obviously, they did not feel the same.

One guy said, "We want to buy a fishing boat and renovate it. We need a place to do that. How about your back yard?"

The second guy said, "We need a place to stay while we do that. We thought that you would let us use your basement. We won't expect anything of you, except a place to do our work and a place to sleep."

She thought—*A giant fishing boat? — Well, at least if there is a natural disaster on this ocean coast, I will have a boat to float and save my children. But, these two guys? The guys who I thought betrayed me? And how do they know so much about the layout of my place. They must have been here without me knowing.*

Regardless of not wanting anything to do with the guys who betrayed her, Mary agreed to their proposal. She was so extremely happy and optimistic about her life that she brought with her the old habit of wanting to share her good fortune with everyone. She wanted to help others the way she had been helped.

A giant fishing boat arrived and filled the back yard. Mary kind of liked it and felt safe with it there considering that she was reading books about changes to the earth. True to their word, the guys worked on their boat. They did track mud through her kitchen and down the stairs instead of always using the outside door to the basement. A former tenant had left an old double bed with mattress in the basement; Mary assumed that they were sleeping on it.

One day a couple of months later, without a word of thanks, the boat and the men were gone.

chapter eight

Cups

Mary had run away to live her own life in her own way and somehow people were finding her and showing up unexpectedly. Mary did not know how she had become a magnet. The house was constantly filled with guests from near and far—some she knew and others were strangers. She continued to believe that God would provide so long as she was looking after everyone. She was still sharing what little she did have.

Mary played her guitar while many a guest just sat on cushions and listened quietly. Mary did not know why they were there, so she simply played on between brief conversations. Then she would fill bowls with soup from a large pot on the stove and hand out bowls to anyone visiting.

Guilt was setting in as her children had less while she continued to care for anyone and everyone who showed up at her door. More and more people were coming and Louise was still there every day, walking right in as though she lived in Mary's home.

Mary's thoughts were—*All my life, I had no interest in amassing material things or money, those things easily slip through my hand and are gone.* She accepted this way of living.

Mary was celibate. In her mind, sex without love was never going to happen again. She wished for love, but it was not happening. No matter who came around, she hosted, but kept to herself.

She had been sleeping. Her eyes opened. In between waking and sleeping she was having a vision: **Two plain looking brown cups float in the air in front of Mary. The cups are of different sizes—one smaller representing female, and one larger representing male. The cups slowly move toward each other. They touch and merge. Simultaneously, Mary felt her body on fire in an intense orgasm. The male and female within her body had fused in blissful, fiery orgasm encompassing her whole body.**

She was laying on her back in bed, feeling the breeze on her face as it blew past the curtain of an open window beside her. She lay wide awake. Nothing like it had ever happened before. The aftermath was of sexual satisfaction, extreme surprise and puzzlement as to why it happened. She wondered if she was being taught something about how we are complete within ourselves.

She turned her face to feel the breeze better. She wondered about spirit, having heard that spirits can take on different genders through incarnations. But, she was not concerned with spirit this time. She was emerging with new knowledge of what it means to be human. Always having thought of herself as female, she now understood for the first time how human bodies do have both genders, one being predominant from conception. This experience turned her attention to the meaning and power of cups. Throughout written history, cups were often mentioned. Mary wondered — *why were cups brought to me in a lucid vision? — were they to show what humans are capable of?*

Only a few days later the cups would play another drama.

Mary had gone to the open window of the living room and reached out to pick a white flower from the tree outside the window. Someone had told her they was orange blossoms, but she wondered about that because to her knowledge the tree never had oranges. It was just loaded with fragrant blossoms that seemed to last a long time. She smelled the blossom in her hand and put it in her long, brown hair just above her ear where she wore flowers often. She could smell them as she went about her day, but more than that, she just liked the feeling of wearing real flowers in her hair.

There was a knock on the door. She opened it to find her friend Bob from the meditation centre standing there with another man. The other man was introduced as Fred.

Fred was silent, seemingly mesmerized at the sight of Mary.

"Come in." Mary asked, "You've come from where?"

"Back east," Bob answered. "To drop in on you."

Mary laughed, "You've traveled thousands of miles to drop in on me?"

She ushered the men in.

"Would you like tea or coffee?" she asked.

The men walked into the living room and while Mary was getting coffee in the kitchen, they stood by the window and looked out. When she came back into the living room, Bob took her hand and placed a stone in her palm. Fred was still silent as he watched.

Mary looked at the large, orange gem in her hand.

Bob explained, "It's a Carnelian. It means that now your true love will come to you."

The men stayed and rolled out sleeping bags in the living room for the night.

The next day Mary took the stone to the man in the Persian Arts shop where she had gone to visit when she first arrived in this city and was enthralled at the atmosphere. She admired how the elderly Persian man gave time and attention to each and every person in his shop. She felt it was a lesson for her, so she watched him intently. At the time, all she could afford was a tiny vial of Wild Rose perfume for one dollar that he had shown her, but that had made her feel extra special.

The Persian man looked at the stone and explained, "A Carnelian stone is believed to hold energy that is connected to sexuality, fertility and the root chakra."

"Can you set it into a ring for me?"

"Yes. I have a ring design for this kind of stone. I suggest 10 karat gold because it is stronger than 14 karat."

He pulled out readymade rings without stones. Mary chose a ring and after a little wait, she walked out with her Carnelian ring.

That evening, with the ring on her finger, she sat on a cushion and played her guitar softly. The children were in and out of the room. Her baby, now a few months old, played beside her on the Persian rug.

Bob and Fred were talking to each other across the room. Mary was not paying attention to them; she was engrossed in her guitar and the music book on the floor in front of her.

During the night when the children were asleep in their rooms, Mary was woken up by footsteps coming up the stairs. Guests were not allowed upstairs. Bob entered her bedroom. He stood just inside the doorway.

He asked, "Mary, can I come in?"

"No. Please leave."

He politely did leave. Mary listened to his footsteps going down the stairs. She fell back to sleep.

Bob rolled back into his sleeping bag, trying to sleep, but Fred was keeping him awake.

Fred was making imaginary circles on the Persian rug. He put on a pointed hat and then lit a candle and held it as he walked in circles chanting Mary's name along with mumbled incantations.

Meanwhile, Mary was having a lucid dream: **A woman in a long dress appeared and spoke to Mary. She said, "Downstairs, Bob's friend Fred is practicing a magical routine that he hopes will bring you to him sexually. You are being warned so that you do not fall under his spell."**

Mary asked, "What will happen if I do fall under his spell?"

"Do not be tempted. The man is not right for you."

Mary woke up. The dream was so real and clear. She dared not go downstairs but stayed wide-eyed in her bed.

The next morning, Bob approached Mary when the children were not close by. "My friend thinks he is in love with you. But you should know that he is trying to seduce you with magic. He stays awake in the night. He makes a circle on the living room rug and walks in circles doing some sort of ceremony that is supposed to make you love him and have sex with him. He has also started to wander around in the daytime, calling your name under his breath. I think you should be aware of this. Mary, I want you. I've come a long way for you."

She looked at him with sympathy.

"Thanks for telling me. I'm not ... uh, I wish for love but I just found me. ... Not yet, Bob, I'm sorry, not now."

Bob looked devastated.

Over the next few hours, Mary thought over a few happenings. For some reason, people were still coming from long distances and locally to check her out. Some people thought she had something to teach. She thought she had nothing to teach so she would play her guitar and serve soup. What really boggled her mind was varying proposals from men. It was beyond her why any man would want to take on a woman with five children. Bob was not the first. One memorable guy named Fish had come from California with a friend and found his way to Mary. He was the old age of nineteen. He started fishing right away to catch Mary. Over several weeks, he tried hard to convince her that a nineteen year old man and thirty year old woman were the most sexually compatible. Mary had been amused at his mathematics and no fish was caught.

Only a few evenings ago, a well known author had plopped himself down beside her for a chat as she sat on her front porch stairs just to watch falling stars. He had come out of nowhere unexpectedly to check her out. She was uninterested in him as a man, so he wandered off after a while.

In the afternoon of Bob's proposal and warning, Mary was coming up the street toward the house with her two babies in the carriage surrounded by bags of groceries. From down the block, she could see Fred out on the street, seemingly waiting for her.

Mary looked away into the distant mountains. She started to silently chant a mantra Bhikhu had taught her. It had always given her energy and strength in times of need.

That evening, Mary was sitting on a cushion on the floor, quietly playing her guitar and ignoring the men in the house. Another man had dropped in to visit and was across the room talking to Bob.

Fred came into the room. Bob and the visitor stopped talking. Odd silence caused Mary to look up.

Fred had come into the room from a different direction than from the kitchen. He was carrying two white mugs from the kitchen — one cup in each hand, held carefully out in front of his chest. His face had a look of determination and purpose. Fred walked directly to Mary and carefully knelt down in front of her. He set the cups down on the rug in front of her.

Mary laid her guitar down on the floor beside her. She could see that the cups had cooking oil in them.

Fred slowly lit a fire in each cup. Slowly, he brought his hands together over the cups and the two fires as though uniting the two flames. He picked up the cups and held them about ten inches apart, one in each hand in front of Mary right at her eye level.

Mary's thoughts raced. Instinctively, she knew what the cups meant. She knew one fire was meant to be her and he was the other. It dawned on her at that moment that she had been given a lesson in a vision about the meaning of these cups. She knew that Fred's intention was to draw the two flames together into one flame and that was to draw her to him in a sexual union.

Fred concentrated hard. His eyes were intensely looking at Mary as he started moving the cups together. His eyes were catching the glow of the fire as he was trying to move the cups together.

Mary was watching the cups. She avoided Fred's eyes. She was in a battle of wills. She was maintaining a serene, innocent exterior while mentally in a battle of her lifetime. She was convinced her whole future depended on this moment. Using all her mental strength, she was determined that the flames would not become one. She concentrated on the cups to keep them apart. The battle was on!

Fred was concentrating so hard that his hands turned white. Veins stood out in his arms. His face was in a tight grimace with flames in his eyes.

Mary's eyes were on the cups. Over a few minutes, she could feel the pressure coming from him. She fought back, determined to hold the cups apart.

The cups were inching closer and near to each other but not yet touching. There was a loud explosion. Flames flew into the air and extinguished in the air. Oil spilled to the floor. Fred held pieces of two broken cups in his hands.

He was shocked. He slumped back on his heels in defeat.

Mary leaned back against the wall in relief.

Fred, defeated and dejected, slowly picked himself up with broken pieces of the cups and left the room without a word.

It was over.

The next day, Mary watched them leave the house with their backpacks and drive away.

She went to the open window in her living room and reached for a flower on the tree. She paused to admire the Carnelian ring on her finger. She picked a flower and smelled it. She placed it in her long hair, just above her ear. She was thankful for the fragrance of the flower and for her freedom to enjoy a new day. She sent up a wish that one day her true, beloved lover would find her.

Soon after Bob and Fred left, Mary found herself in a taxi with Edith, her old friend from the meditation centre. Again, Mary wondered how people were making their way to her because she did not even have a telephone. But here she was — Edith.

"I'm his forerunner. Bhikhu is on his way to see you. He's coming from Thailand. He's been ordained a Llama. He'll be here tomorrow. He wants you to assemble people for a meeting."

Mary settled Edith into her children's bedroom. There was no furniture in the room, just a mattress on the floor, but Edith was okay with it.

Mary apologized, "Travelers always roll out their sleeping bags in the living room. You deserve privacy. Sorry, this is all I have to offer. My daughter will sleep with me."

The next day Mary opened the door to the Bhikhu standing there in saffron robes that were fuller and more prestigious than his previous robes. A tall saffron hat was on his head.

Some of the people who had been hanging around in Mary's living room the past while, now sat in anticipation of what she was offering in this invitation to be present. Louise was among the group.

Bhikhu took the only chair in the room. The chair was an orange upholstered, old relic with no armrests and had no legs, so it sat low. He sat on it, not minding because he was used to sitting in the lotus position. His large stature in his large robes looked majestic as he covered the chair.

He sat silently, surveying the people in the room. His eyes slowly moved from one person to the next. People tried to be still, but they began to squirm.

Mary stood in the doorway to the kitchen, watching the Bhikhu survey the people.

He spoke, "Instead of a discourse, I wish to see each of you by yourself."

Each person filed out and back into the room one by one. After the interview, the person exited the house looking somewhat bewildered, except for Louise who needed to be in on everything that happened to Mary.

As the last person exited, Bhikhu rose and towered over Mary.

"Mary, you need to use discrimination. There is a difference between helping the needy and helping people to be selfish and lazy."

Bhikhu handed Mary a Fire Opal embedded in the side of yellow stone carved in the shape of a pyramid.

Louise had a baby boy. A few weeks later her parents crossed the country to take her and their grandchild home. Along with Louise leaving, so did almost all of Mary's clothes and other items that Louise had coveted. Mary was freed of her, but had almost nothing to wear for a second time.

chapter nine

Husband Three

Mary was vacuuming her Persian rug and decided to do something else for a minute. When she turned back to the vacuum cleaner, she saw that the cord had made a perfect treble clef in the middle of the rug. Her first impression was that someone who is musical will come into her life. Then she got on with her work and thought about it as imagination that meant nothing.

She had been telling herself—*I am not going out looking for love. If it is to come to me, it will find me.* She felt assured that love would come knocking on her door.

A few days after that thought, it was a sunny autumn day when Mary was walking along the street with two of her children in the baby carriage. She was feeling especially good and felt like she was shining in the sunshine.

Her toddler daughter was now talking. "Look, the sun's hanging out."

Mary was just happily enjoying how her child chose to say what she was seeing when a car stopped beside her. Carolyn, a friend from the coffee house days was in the driver's seat. After a marriage breakup, she also landed in the same area by the beach to start over.

She shouted, "Hi, I want you to meet my friend."

Introduction to the male friend was made and then Mary walked on thinking nothing more about it. She was headed to the beach for a while and then back home to cook dinner for her school children.

As an evening snack, Mary made wheat cereal roasted with a heavy coating of garlic powder, salt and oil. She was enjoying time with no people other than her children. She expected no one, so she felt free to indulge in garlic and just spend time playing her guitar for her own enjoyment. She was marvelling that she now could play a piece of music that she had admired a friend playing and wished she could.

She was stinking of garlic to high heaven when there was a knock on the door.

She was surprised to find the man she was introduced to earlier standing there.

He started the conversation. "Hello. I saw you walking down the street today. I asked Carolyn to stop the car and introduce us. Can I come in?"

"Of course, come in."

They spent an evening sitting on cushions over the Persian rug and just talked. He had a PhD and had been teaching in Mary's home town, so they had friends in common. A couple of hours later, he left. The impression left with Mary was that he was possibly the most interesting of all the men who had sought a relationship with her.

He returned the following day with a guy Mary knew, who had been a patron of the old coffee house. It turned out he and Paul knew each other because of Paul's teaching at the university after Mary had left town. The men talked mostly with each other about how this was the start of their world tour. After an hour of visiting and giving Mary's oldest son a camera, they were gone.

Mary thought nothing more about it until she learned that after the guys left her house, Paul abandoned his trip around the world. Instead he went back to his home town.

Mary was not expecting to see Paul again, but a couple of months later, there was another knock on her door.

Mary opened it to find Paul standing there looking especially tired. He stepped in. They hugged.

The hug felt flat. Mary was disappointed because she was keenly aware that she felt nothing special for Paul. She had hoped for more if she ever saw him again, but it was not there.

He explained he had just been driving thousands of miles with no sleep to come back to her.

What a surprise! Mary now felt obligated and welcomed him into her house with uneasiness.

He stayed, and stayed, and stayed. He seemed to not want to leave and soon, as weeks went by, they were like a couple living together. Regardless of the flat feelings, he was interesting.

He was out of work, so he decided to use his spare time to follow a passion he had harboured. He wanted to play the flute. So with what money he still had, he bought a silver flute and found a flutist that played in the symphony to teach him. Then he stood every day on the Persian rug where the cord had made a treble clef and practiced his flute.

Mary thought things were going okay—she had a musician in the house. Several weeks after he came, Mary found out Paul was grieving another woman who jilted him. She had come home after grocery shopping one afternoon to find him in crisis. He had punched a hole in her bedroom wall and the beads from a water-pearl necklace her brother had given her were strewn all over the room. He was in tears.

She was shocked at the scene.

He exclaimed, "My girlfriend disappeared. I couldn't find her. I want to commit suicide."

Mary responded with a gut feeling, "So, do what you want."

She walked away.

She surprised herself with her reaction. This was the first she knew about another woman. She felt defiled. She felt he had betrayed her.

This was the first time in her life that she acted this way to anyone.

It shocked Paul. He immediately recovered as if nothing happened.

To her surprise, he never mentioned the other woman again and never pulled the suicide act again. It was as though it never happened.

Mary had allowed this man to stay and become a member of the household. Her children were looking to him hopefully as a father. She was in a dilemma of whether or not to kick him out. It was easiest just to let it go for a day, then another day while she was not happy.

He took the family to an archaeology dig that was in progress not far from the city. It excited the children, especially the oldest daughter. After that, one day just led to more days.

Paul decided that he needed to go back the Vermont, where he left his precious red canvas canoe. He wanted to get it and invited Mary to make the trip across the country with him.

The children were left half way with Mary's parents. It was the first time Mary had time away from her children. It was the first time in many years that she had an alone time with a man. It was an enjoyable trip until they came to Paul's parents' home.

What she did not count on was Paul's parents' rejection of her. They objected to her because she had five children — she was obviously after the money he did not have, or family money they did have — she was not Jewish — she had a German name — Mary lived across the country and was taking their precious son away. Paul's mother was determined not to talk with Mary and gave her the silent treatment. Paul's father paced the floor, very upset over a reminder of his sister who died in a German concentration camp.

During the visit of a few days while Paul seemed okay about the visit, Mary was eyed with suspicion and watched like a criminal. Mary could see the parents' blatant discomfort. She sympathized, but in her innocence it was extremely uncomfortable to be treated with such disdain for crimes she had not and would not commit.

When the parents were out of the house, Paul searched the bathroom closet to see if his mother still needed menstruation pads. Somehow, he was tangled unhealthily with his mother.

When Paul and Mary were leaving a few days later, Paul's mother had gone shopping or deliberately left the house, refusing to say goodbye. Paul and his father were talking by the car. Mary was in the house alone, not wanting to interrupt the father and son. It was the first time she was in a house with a piano since her childhood. She had been yearning to play it. She could not resist the opportunity to play it while waiting to leave.

When she realized it must be time to get into the car, she went out. Paul's father retreated to the house as soon as she came out. Then he immediately came running back out, exclaiming the piano lamp was missing.

Mary was shocked. She knew he was accusing her of stealing. Paul went back into the house. In a few minutes he came out and got into the car without a word.

Mary asked, "What happened?"

"The lamp was behind the piano. The housekeeper must have put it there."

Mary knew it had been hidden there because it had been on the piano when she was in the house. No more was said.

On the way back, Mary and Paul enjoyed canoeing in lakes. Mary did not have a bathing suit, so she simply took off her shirt and canoed in her pink bra, something she never would have done in the past. It was somehow freeing to just let go of past barriers and be so relaxed.

Back in Mary's home town, they visited old friends that they knew in common from the coffee house days and the university crowd that Paul knew from the job he left. That's when Mary learned that Paul had been fired for adultery with his boss's wife. More than that, Paul had been living in their home, so he did it in the boss's own home. Paul's only excuse was that the wife enticed him by laying a doll on his bed with its legs wide open.

It was a dinner invitation that led to the meeting with another professor. Paul and Mary were huddled around a small kitchen table, eating a spaghetti dinner in the home of Ted and Marianne. He taught at the university. She was a dancer. When they finished eating, Ted jumped up and took giant steps toward the piano in the next room which was a dining room with only a black, grand piano. He launched into playing loudly. Marianne jumped up and ran into the adjoining living room. Mary and Paul followed and sat on wooden chairs. The rooms were bare except for the black grand piano and the few wooden chairs along one wall. Marianne floated around on bare, shining, golden wood floors.

The telephone rang. Ted jumped up, ran to the hallway and answered.

"Oh, sure. Come on over."

He came back explaining that Ben and his family were stopping by; that they had been on holidays and were just stopping by before heading home.

A few minutes later, a family arrived. In came a woman followed by two small boys, followed by the father.

After introductions, the mother took a chair and loudly held court. Her voice filled all space.

The father followed his boys who wandered around aimlessly in the bare home. Mary got out of her chair and followed because she would rather talk to the father than to the loud mouthed mother. But, the father just kept to himself and ignored Mary. She simply gave up trying to get to know him.

Mary's parents were very accepting of Paul in the few days while picking up the children. They were joyful with the children and wanted to keep them. Their thoughts were that Mary could go back and live with Paul or whoever while the children, especially the oldest children, could stay in a stable home with grandparents. Mary realized her way of life and problems had the effect on her parents that she was being judged as footloose and fancy free. Mary panicked. She wanted her children and would have to rip them away from her parents again. She had an argument with her mother in the garden. It was the first time Mary had tears in front of anyone. In the past, she had never allowed herself to be that vulnerable in front of anyone, even her parents, but this time she could not control the tears. Mary was adamant that all the children were leaving with her. Her mother relented.

In a campground on the way home, while the children were playing and Paul seemed to be off on his own, Mary sat on a log wondering where Ben was and why she was still thinking about him. Somehow, Ben had made an unforgettable impression on her.

Meanwhile, Mary was unaware that while visiting with his own parents, Paul had promised he would take Mary and her children back to the coast and then he would leave them. He was out of a job and broke, so he made a promise to himself — if he found a job right away, he would stay with the family—if not, he would head back to his own family and to his heartbroken mother.

They arrived home. The next day there was a knock on the door. A grey haired man that seemed to shine from head to toe and was dressed in a neatly pressed Harris Tweed jacket was standing there with a big smile.

Seated on Mary's cushions on the Persian rug, he explained that he had come to speak with Paul because he was a professor from the university and wanted to hire Paul to teach. He explained to Paul that he had read Paul's PhD thesis and decided to search for him.

Mary was astounded because there was no telephone in the house and here was another person arriving with a special mission.

The men talked and Paul was hired on the spot.

It came as a complete surprise when Paul told Mary of his plan to leave if he had no job, but he would now stay.

Because of another strange happening that Mary wondered about, she was now invited to be the common-law wife of a university professor. She decided to continue out of curiosity.

Her old house was not to the liking of Paul, who had never before experienced a life of want or living in a crummy old house. He rented a big, furnished house in a forest with a river running past the green lawn. The house had big windows overlooking the fast running river that had the soothing sound of running water all the time, and was especially relaxing at night while sleeping.

It was suitable for a university professor, but Mary was not used to so much. She felt guilty about all the people in the world who did not have so much. It was a house that the children enjoyed.

Paul found an old upright piano that had been refurbished and surprised Mary when it was delivered to her. He came across a concert harp that was being sold by a professor at the university and bought it for Mary. The harp satisfied a lifelong dream she had and that he had not even known about — she wondered what angels had heard her wish because she had never mentioned it to anyone. Paul bought a shiny new guitar for her that had the fullness of sound that she had craved. Her son had a violin and violin lessons. Her other son experimented with flute and then settled on an electric guitar.

Paul was by no mean rich, in fact it was a moderate lifestyle, but it was more than Mary's family had ever had. The family was flourishing. It was a lifestyle that Paul was used to, where children had music lessons and dance lessons, and camping in the summers. Personally, Mary was experiencing a lifestyle that she never expected to afford in her wildest dreams. The house was filled with music and dance in every room. The house was a fulfilment of Mary's best wishes. All other concerns about being loved went out the window.

Living at the foot of a mountain, the family was outfitted with skis and could go skiing anytime. The boys were enjoying a life like Mary had never imagined. The little children enjoyed sitting in a backpack on Paul's back as he maneuvered around the mountain. Mary learned to ski.

They took holidays to cross-country ski in resorts around the province. They canoed rivers and lakes around the province.

There were bicycle outings. Paul bought a van and outfitted it to carry many bicycles. They travelled by ferry and bicycled the many islands on many different Sundays. The little girls rode around in seats on Paul's and Mary's bicycles while the three older children rode their own bicycles.

They camped on the beach of the outer coast of the province where there was a new kind of freedom in the wild, wide open ocean as the tides came and went.

The family took a trip south to the Grand Canyon and to visit old ruins of another culture. They camped out under the stars because it was so warm. They saw stars in a deep turquoise sky and comets that all seemed closer to the earth than up north. They ate food of the southern native people.

Paul was making an effort to be a real member of the family and encouraged all the activities. Mary organized family reunions on her brother's farm. (Her brother had married, bought a farm to start a new lifestyle and had children.)

Amidst all the activities, Mary had two pregnancies with extreme nausea twenty-four hours a day. The first pregnancy ended in a miscarriage at four and a half months. Paul was happy because he had suggested an abortion anyway.

It was followed in the same year by a second pregnancy. Paul's parents came to visit. Mary was instructed by Paul's mother that she was to keep the pregnancy a secret and definitely Mary was not to upset Paul's father with a pregnancy. Mary would lay out of sight on the cold bathroom floor for relief from pretending she was okay. She suffered a miscarriage at five and a half months.

On a following visit, as the family and Paul's parents were taking a walk together, Paul's mother rushed to Mary's side, leaving her husband behind to walk with Paul.

She asked, "When are you going to have Paul's baby?"

This question angered Mary. She knew the woman had been told about the miscarriage.

Mary quipped over her shoulder, "Never!" And she kept walking, feeling that now she had gotten even with the woman who had made her life miserable.

It was Christmas time. Paul's parents had brought small, inexpensive gifts for everyone, but nothing for Mary. On Christmas Eve, Mary was setting the table in the dining room for the big celebration meal that she had cooked for the event because Christmas Eve was special in her family tradition. Mary was lighting candles on the table when Paul's mother sidled up to her.

She said, "My friends tell me that since you have not disappeared in seven years, I should accept you."

Mary did not respond. She continued getting the table ready, but the statement burned even if she knew it all along. It was ironic because every time Paul's parents came to visit, and it was at least once a year, they slept in Mary's bed and Mary had to sleep on a sofa. After seven years of this, Paul's mother was going to accept her? Mary did not believe it.

The relationship with Paul took the family to living in an Inuit village over one winter. Paul went ahead. Mary and the children followed.

She lined up the excited children and their luggage at the airport. Having no suitcases, she had packed Mexican grass baskets with their belongings. It was a colorful scene. They had never been on an airplane before, and now they were going on several planes, including a bubble float plane from the Second World War that would take them on the last leg north.

Halfway, they were stopped overnight along the Hudson Bay. The children had their first introduction to making friends with Inuit boarding school children. They all ate in a cafeteria that had loads of food. Mary had never before experienced such a feast that she did not have to cook for her family except when the kids were with her own parents or at family reunions. It was a fun stay overnight.

When it was time to leave the next day, the word was that the bubble plane was broken. After another layover, that afternoon the kids came running to tell Mary that they had been watching the pilots fix the plane with tape, "kind of like bandaids," they said excitedly, and now it was time to fly. She needed to run and off they went.

The small plane had a few Inuit women passengers and Mary's family. Mary's seat swayed back and forth by several inches. With a clear view all around, the scenery below was pure white with many white potholes that were frozen lakes. Above was blue sky. It was surreal.

Arriving, they swooped down, crashing through a thin layer of ice into the water that splashed up to swallow the plane. Then it surfaced and floated to land. Inuit men were waiting to help everyone get onto land and to carry luggage to the houses. On the way from the dock to the house, Inuit children followed Mary's family. They pretended to walk like white people walk, which was hilarious to them and to Mary.

They had arrived just in time because, then there was freeze-up. Eight weeks of no planes coming or going—no food delivery of any kind. What was in the village was all there was. People fished and hunted for food. Mary was told it was a year of famine because hunting was not so good.

Mary walked with her children to the waterfront where women and children were fishing. As the fish were brought out of the water, the children ate the fish—fresh.

Mary's children learned about another culture while melding into the lives and homes of Inuit children of their ages.

The church was a small building that smelled strongly of seal. The Anglican church was more successful than Catholic partly because politically, the Catholic priest had lost the trust of the people. He had betrayed them in hearings in the South.

Mary quickly developed an artistic relationship with a well-known Inuit artist. Two artists meeting while enjoying the artistry of the universe! She met him the night she was just walking to enjoy the northern lights. He was on the roof of his small house, doing the same thing. Being on his roof brought him just that much closer to northern lights that were more brilliant with color than Mary had ever seen. The whole sky was in colorful sheaths of motion. The sound was like a magic musical concert with full orchestra. She had not known the aurora borealis made such loud music.

He invited her to come the next day into his studio that he shared with other artists. She loved his work and took a liking to two of his large prints on rice paper, but did not let him know that she had a special affinity to them.

Christmas Day, he came running through the snow with two prints rolled up in his hands and gave them to Mary. He explained that one was about bounty and the other was famine. He was so happy in giving to Mary. She was thinking it a miracle that this special man was giving her his precious prints, and how did he even know how much she loved them?

The people of the village were generous. Sharing was a way of life. Mary's house had a freezer packed full with fish. When a caribou was killed at Christmas time, a roast of caribou was delivered to Mary's family for Christmas dinner.

Then, a polar bear was killed and a roast was delivered to Mary. It stunk so much that Mary marinaded it and put it in the refrigerator. It stunk so much that even though it was refrigerated, its stink permeated the whole house. Mary could not cook it. She had to give it back. Then she had to look at the bear hide hanging on the wall of the community centre. The white fur was covered in fleas that jumped around. But, more than that, Mary was living where people needed to kill to survive. There were no plants to live off of. There was a time of year when there were no airplanes coming and going. It was kill or starve.

Walking on the outskirts of the village, Mary picked a few dried weeds out of the snow to take home and put in a vase. She realized in the midst of endless ice and snow that her roots were as a farmer, not a hunter and gatherer. Where she was standing, so far away from her life as she knew it on earth, it seemed like she could be on the moon.

The first airplane that arrived after eight week of freeze-up, brought a plane load of Orange Crush and absolutely no food for the Bay store. People were disappointed. Mary realized that the people of the village would starve if they depended on the white men of the south who apparently had no idea that people need food and not Orange Crush.

Some of the school teachers were having the time of their lives. The men were targets for single women of the village who wanted them for whatever reason — like sexually or a better lifestyle, or just because the men were from the south and maybe white. Often babies had been born and left behind as the men just went south. A female teacher had to be flown south by Christmas because of the isolation that she could not handle.

There were underlying differences in ways of living that Mary became aware of. She became aware of the trading of babies. When a baby was born, it might stay in its birth family. The baby might also be given to another family for paying debt, to glean a favor, or to grow up as a slave to one of more members of the adoptive family. Mary was bothered about the slave children and she had no idea how many adults were slaves in the village and across the northern country.

Mary, a lifelong animal lover, made friends with a Husky puppy that came around her house just to be friendly. One afternoon there was a commotion outside. She went out to find the local policeman in uniform with a long gun in his hands. He was chasing something around her house. As Mary came out, the little puppy appeared from under her house with its jaw shot off. The puppy was looking for help. Mary screamed and screamed at the policeman. The children were out of school for recess just across the road. They stopped playing as the children looked over to what was happening. Mary's own daughter was among the children.

What was happening was that the policeman had been asked to kill the puppy for its fur. The school children thought Mary was upset because she thought the policeman was going to shoot her. The children had no understanding that Mary would be upset over a dog being shot and running around with no jaw while trying to look for protection from Mary.

The puppy and its cruel death would forever bother Mary, no matter how long she would live.

Mary's son had been taken out on a skidoo with some men to hunt. They built a snow house on the land and taught Mary's son how they lived out on the land. He came back during a winter storm covered in a thick layer of snow. Mary had been frightened about his wellbeing, so when he arrived home it was an extreme relief.

Then, the younger brother to one of the men was jealous about the hunting trip that he had not been invited on. He was also jealous over a girl that liked Mary's son, and he was also jealous because Mary's son had respect for his work with men of the village delivering water to households. The boy had a history of mental disturbances, so one evening following the hunting trip, the fourteen year old boy entered a house where Mary's sons were visiting with friends. Mary's son was sitting on the top bunk of a bed. The disturbed boy threw a knife at Mary's son. The knife was thrown with proficiency at close range straight at his heart. Instinctively, Mary's son lifted his arm to protect his heart. His wrist caught the knife. He had to be taken to the onsite nurse to have his wrist stitched.

That was enough. The children were not safe. They would keep friendships and fond memories for a lifetime, but it was time to leave. The next day, the policeman arrived at Mary's home to tell her that he could not promise round the clock protection, verifying that it was time to leave the village.

Paul was away in another village so Mary and the children were leaving him behind to complete his work. It was an evening flight. A large, sleek, white airplane, not a bubble plane, was waiting on a white, icy runway. Baskets of belongings were already loaded. Mary and the children were at the edge of the village and being told by the attendant to hurry. A young woman with a baby on her back approached Mary.

"I want to go with you. Please help me. I am a slave to an old blind man. This is his baby."

Mary was stunned. Her imagination of the hell this woman must be living in raced through her mind. Her plane tickets for the family were being paid for by government. She had absolutely no money to buy a flight ticket for the woman and the baby. In fact, even if a bank was open, Mary had no bank account to draw money from. Mary needed to deny the woman's request and left her standing there.

The children were ahead of Mary as the plane waited. Mary started running to catch up. She was so upset that she lost her footing and slipped on the ice, landing on her hip.

Mary's hip hurt for months, reminding her of the woman she had to leave behind. In the horror of the moment of realizing she could not help, Mary had not even gotten the woman's name, and she had never seen her around the village to know who her friends were, so she could not send for her and know that the right woman would arrive. More than that, the Catholic priest was the intake of all mail. He thought it was his mission to go through everyone's mail and decide who got what. Some of the mail, according to his judgment, just never made it to the person the mail was sent to.

The memory of the slave woman and her baby was never going to leave Mary.

Back home again, Mary was reading a book about Terisa of Avila. The next morning as daylight was breaking, she was woken up part way …

Between waking and sleeping, Mary was in a state where she was dreaming—that she was dreaming—that she was dreaming. She went through three levels to deeper levels of consciousness—to a state of super consciousness. She was more acutely awake than ordinary every day awake consciousness. She heard a choir of a thousand, thousand angels singing, more beautiful and powerful than she

could describe and more beautiful than anything on earth.

Soon after, she had another astral travel experience. She was in bed when three men appeared: **Albert Einstein flanked by Beethoven and Mozart were extremely large so that only their heads and a little of their chests were visible to Mary. Einstein took Mary out of her body into his hand. She was tiny on the palm of his hand. Again, walls were not there. He carried her into space. Traveling in space, they passed a few other beings. Mary's mother was out of body and watched with interest as they passed by. Mary's youngest daughter was simply floating around while reading a book. Mary was pleased because her daughter was just beginning to read and Mary now knew that her daughter would soon be reading proficiently because she could do so in her astral body.**

At the chosen destination, Mary and Einstein were suddenly the same size, standing on the edge of a city that was similar to a city on earth, but it was somewhere in space. As they looked in at the city, Einstein talked a long time. He was giving Mary a lesson about life ...

Mary was placed back into her physical body fast. She lay in bed trying to remember the lesson Einstein had just given her. She could remember the trip vividly and the faces of the men vividly, the look of the city vividly, and her mother and child vividly, but nothing of the teaching given to her.

Later that day, a man dropped by to visit with Paul. The man considered himself a guru, so Mary sat down with the men and tried to describe her experience of a few hours ago.

The room was absolutely silent. Mary waited. There was no response from the visitor or from Paul. Their faces were blank. In the lack of response, Mary felt stupid for telling her story. She thought they believed she was delusional. She left the room vowing not to tell anyone ever again about her experiences.

Paul never did talk with Mary about any of her experiences. In fact, he never talked with her about anything. He never asked her about her thoughts or wishes, or even how her day went. There was little communication. Family life was a matter of doing each day of breakfast and dinner with snacks, and lunches in between. They were either going to work or going on trips and even on trips, he did not talk with Mary.

Dinner was always a full table setting with a table cloth and candles that stood in the middle of a table surrounded by a family eating healthy home cooked meals. That was a time for catching up on what was happening with the children, but Paul never talked with Mary over dinner.

Meanwhile, Mary was always feeling lonely. Daily life had no intimacy with Paul. He sat at his desk and pretended to be working all the time, except for meals and bicycle trips where Mary followed behind him as he raced along. Or, they went skiing and again she was not skiing with him because he always went on trails she could not manage. It was cross country skiing where she shined and could keep up.

During this time, the boys came running into the kitchen to say they had seen James driving by the house. A few minutes later the telephone rang. Mary answered to hear James' voice.

"Hi Mary. I've missed you."

"Get lost!" was Mary's response.

"Clean your cup!" he shouted at her.

Mary hung up on him. She felt angry that he, of all people, would tell her to clean her cup. He had not asked about the children so she felt justified about telling him to get lost and not invite him into her life again. In fact, she was convinced that he wanted a place to stay while in town and she was having none of it.

The relationship behind the scenes between the children and Paul had become increasingly testy, especially as the children grew older. Paul seemed to have a hard time with growing boys. Behind Mary's back he was insulting and constantly make the boys feel inferior to himself.

Paul was suddenly refusing the father role. He wanted to be called by his first name only and not referred to as a father. Behind Mary's back he did not allow pets in the house. Mary wondered why the cat was always outside. Behind Mary's back he made life with all the children difficult. With Mary, he pretended everything was okay.

After being in the family for years, it was an enlightening day when he came home from work and the eight year old daughter greeted him by saying, "Hi, Dad."

"Don't call me dad!" he blew up at her as he came through the doorway.

The eleven year old daughter objected to his attitude. He smacked her. She ran into the bathroom to get away. He followed and knocked her into the bathtub. It was the first time he actually hit one of the children.

Following that day he asked Mary to go for a walk in the park. They were surrounded by magnificent trees, deep in the park when he stopped. He turned to Mary and asked, "Can we be like we used to be?"

The question was a puzzle to Mary – *why now? – what was it like that he wants back?*

Paul grabbed Mary, hugging her and planting a kiss intended for her lips. He had big lips and opened his mouth as her kissed her. She felt a wet slobber covering the lower part of her face. She recoiled.

He recoiled in response and just looked at her.

Mary had no way of explaining why she recoiled. She did not want to insult him by telling him he did not know how to kiss. It dawned on her that they never did kiss in all their years together. They walked on in silence. She knew that she had damaged the relationship beyond repair.

One afternoon, Paul did not go to work so that he and Mary could go by themselves to cross country ski on the local mountain. Mary was ahead of him as they came down a hill. She stopped at the bottom and turned to watch him come down. Instead of the trail, he decided to try a jump off the small cliff. He jumped and landed flat on his face in the snow close to Mary's feet.

Mary was silent but bursting with laughter on the inside. He was not finding it funny. He got up and pretended nothing happened. She thought it was a great comedy. She would still find it funny and never stop laughing about it for many years.

It turned out that Paul was having an affair with another woman. His walk in the park and planting a kiss on Mary was his exploration about staying or going. When he had asked about being the way they were and she wondered what it was about—she now had the answer. He was going as a result of Mary's reaction to his slobbering kiss.

When he announced the other woman to Mary, something inside her said, "Don't say it."

She said it. "Why don't you just go and live with her?" As soon as it was out, she regretted saying it.

He said, "I will."

Mary ran out of the house to the nearby park and had a good cry. Life was changing again and she had no idea how the children would take it. Once again, they would be entirely dependent on her because she would never stoop so low as to ask for support from him.

When Mary found out who the woman was, she was not surprised. The woman was a younger version of his own mother—same coloring—same body type—same lots of wrinkles on her face—same attitude of thinking she was better than everyone else.

Before he would leave, he wanted to attend one more family reunion and pretend nothing had changed. Mary went along with it, pretending nothing had changed, except that she was longingly looking at all the married couples with envy and wondering why she could never have a stable life with a man or a home.

Another of his going away wishes, was to take Mary on a holiday to a place by the ocean where there were cabins with no window or doors—open to the warm summer air with beds inside. The setting would have been romantic except for the foreboding of lifestyle changes in days to come.

They canoed on the ocean. Mary was aware that on every canoe trip, she had done all the paddling while he sat at the rear with his paddle simply steering the canoe and he did absolutely no paddling. Even on this final holiday on the ocean with high waves, she looked behind and there he sat at leisure letting her do all the work.

Later on a bicycle ride on the dirt road by the resort, he as usual was ahead of Mary. She caught up to him to ask an important question.

"Why are you leaving me and still hang around for weeks doing all these things together before you leave?"

His answer stunned her. "She owns a house and you don't."

After all the years together, that statement topped them all.

One morning, two months later as the sun rose, he got out of bed, picked up a small bag and left the house, leaving most of his clothing still in the house along with absolutely everything else he owned. Over the next weeks, he would use the things left behind as an excuse to enter into the house unannounced at any time to pick up this and that. He often came at dinner time and sat at the table as though he lived there. One dinner time, he seated himself beside Mary at the table and while they were eating, she became increasingly upset; her hands became numb and disappeared—a phenomenon she would later find out was a sign of severe distress. That was when she asked him not to come to dinner unless he was invited. That upset him, but he was never invited.

Another relationship was over. The children were elated that Paul was gone. Mary had not realized the children had become that unhappy with him around. After he left and she heard stories, Mary was to wonder how she could have been so blind. Paul had been able to keep his behaviour a secret from Mary for many years. He had been one man for the children and another for Mary. After all, he had been a master manipulator.

Then he wanted to come back.

"If I live separately, can I have you both?" he asked over the telephone while Mary was at work.

Mary blew up. "Never! No! Never! I won't have you passing a venereal disease to me. She is not to be trusted. She thinks free sex is where it is at. She will not be faithful to you. That's your problem! Not mine! No! Never! Get lost!"

The walls were thin. The whole building went silent. Mary did not care. As far as she was concerned, it was over and the world could know.

It had been ten years since they had moved from her beach house to the river house. On moving into the river house, Mary had a strong premonition that the relationship would be ten years long. It was.

chapter ten

Fourth by Default

Thinking, enough is enough, Mary was convinced that there could be no fourth marriage of any kind.

Mary's teenaged daughters were critical of her. They were determined to do better, regardless of Mary giving them music lessons and dance lessons while she went without buying new clothes or personal things just so they could have the best training. They talked about finding that one love and one marriage and a better in-law family where the parents of their husbands would still be married in that one loving marriage. They talked about having better careers than Mary.

Mary's sons were more accepting and understanding of what Mary had done to take care of them in the midst of so many problems and unfaithful men.

"Don't get together with a half married man."

This was the advice given to Mary by a medium who claimed to give messages from spirits. He claimed that Mary's uncle John was present along with her son, giving the advice.

Mary had been at loose ends and visited the medium. She wondered—*how did he know I had an uncle John?*—*how did he know I lost a baby boy that lived for four hours?*

Later Mary would wonder if the baby boy was her lost baby or was John her uncle in the present and her son of a past life. The thought was then dismissed. She did not want to indulge in such thoughts, she had a life to live.

It bothered her that the medium had given a message from her uncle John and son. She kept analyzing it. When her grandfather died years earlier, she was a child. At the time, he was living in another province, so Mary did not attend a funeral. She was sympathetic to her mother who was grieving. When her uncle John passed unexpectedly as a young man, Mary was an adult questioning who she was. She burned candles for forty days because she understood that at forty days, he would move on in spirit. On the fortieth day, Mary had a lucid dream: **Her grandfather was at the top of a very long staircase which came out of the sky. Uncle John was at the bottom of the staircase, his back toward Mary as he was looking upward to his father. Mary's grandfather came down the stairway. As he was midway, he looked at Mary to answer her question. His eyes looked deep into Mary as he said, "Get on with your life." He then put his hand out to his son, John and led him up the stairway.** The dream ended when they reached the top of the stairs. Mary's question was answered without an answer.

Meanwhile, Ben who Mary had first met many years ago, had been living in a house down the block with his family.

He and Mary had a casual relationship that was simply occasional greetings. His marriage broke up. Her common-law marriage ended. They both moved away and lost contact.

Mary had become a lay midwife and medical assistance. She was working the emergency hours of a medical clinic for a regular income. Ben, who was a physician, found her there and hired her to work with him as assistant while she continued midwifery. They simply had a working relationship because he made it no secret that he loved his sons and felt a responsibility to them more than wanting any new relationship. That meant, he would be forever tied to his ex-wife. His sons disapproved of him starting any new relationship, and made it absolutely obvious to Mary. In fact, they were downright rude to her.

Ben was definitely a half married man.

Mary's children liked Ben. They thought he was a good and generous man, and welcomed him at all times.

Mary's middle daughter was only sixteen when she ran off to live with a young man who was a twin. They rented an apartment but his twin sister moved in with them right away. Because Mary's daughter needed to contribute financially to the household, Mary invited her to train with her as a medical assistant for which she would be paid. For a few months, it seemed to work out. Then, the daughter was pregnant. The jealous twin sister was interfering in her brother's relationship. It became intolerable. Mary's daughter was now a pregnant teenager with nowhere to live. All her dreams of doing better than Mary were over. Of course, Mary took her in.

The baby was born in a successful home birth with midwife friends attending, hired and paid for by Ben.

Ben decided to buy Mary's daughter a new bicycle with a baby carrier to tow behind the bike. She went to the shop with Ben and met another man. He was twenty years older than her, but she liked him and started to date him, and then disappeared for overnights.

On meeting him, Mary took a dislike to the seemingly dirty man. He was gruff—not nice.

In a fatherly way, Ben wanted to know what his intentions were about a teenaged girl with a baby. He called a meeting. The man came to Mary's house and immediately launched into angry insults at both Mary and Ben, and then about Mary's pictures on the wall. He challenged Ben to a physical fight. Ben sat on the floor to show he was not going to fight and tried to calm the guy.

The man's intention were not revealed in the meeting.

Mary's daughter said she wanted to live on her own, but she went to live with the older man.

Ben wanted a new bicycle so that he could ride with Mary. He went to the bicycle shop again which was the closest in the neighborhood. The same man sold Ben an expensive bike.

Then Mary was babysitting the baby. To return the child to his mother, Ben decided to attach the baby carrier left behind to his new bicycle. It was to be his first time using the new bike. Ben rode the bike with the carrier until they came to a steep hill. He decided to walk it and wheel the bike beside him. That's when he discovered his bicycle had no brakes. On examination, it was discovered that he had been sold a bike with the brake wires cut, so he had no brakes. It was obviously intended to harm Ben. If he had ridden down the hill with no brakes, he and the baby might have been killed either by a roll over or by hitting a moving car. It was obvious that the man who Mary's daughter was living with was dangerous.

The man's next step was to demand money from Mary. He launched into trying to extract money from family members.

Mary told him, "If you wanted a dowry, you should have made that clear at the start."

Mary meant it as a critical joke. It was enough to ban her from seeing her grandchild and her daughter.

Brainwashing of a teenaged girl was easy for the man who had many years experience of being a wayward kid, which was something Mary would learn from his parents who were decent people but dismayed at their son and how he manipulated people. Mary's daughter suddenly did not want anything to do with her own family.

They moved to a remote island. Now he had complete control. Mary's daughter and her child had no access to her family. Next, he took her to a Psychologist living on the island where false memories were instilled and she was told that her 'abusive' family was all wrong for her.

Then there was an island wedding. Neither his family nor Mary's family were present. Now Mary's daughter was legally tied to the man who continued trying to extort money from the family by threatening letters. No one was safe from his wrath when he was refused money.

Mary's daughter and her children (now she had two) suffered abuse that was verbal and very physical, especially for the first born son. His brutality on the boy would have severe consequences that would be long lasting, affecting his teenage years drastically.

Then one day, Mary saw her daughter come out of a hairdressing shop. She had cut her hair. She had worn her hair long to her waist since she was a child. Now it was short just below her ears. Intuition told Mary that her daughter was changing her life. Perhaps she was leaving the older man.

Sure enough, Mary's daughter did divorce the man at the time of the haircut, but the damage was done and could never be erased.

As a divorced single parent, Mary's daughter was starting over. Being seemingly a knockoff of Mary in survival skills, she was enrolled in school again. Being the intelligent person she was, she continued to build on her education over many years and became a physician. The only satisfaction Mary had, was that she thought she might have given her daughter a little of the grounding needed to go on and become a professional in whatever her choice was to be.

Regardless of many overtures by Mary and family members, the daughter never did return to the family. Just as predicted when she was still growing in Mary's womb, there was nothing Mary could do to change it.

The whole heartbreaking loss of her daughter and grandchildren had Mary wondering — *how much do we bring with us from previous lives — certainly, my daughter's behaviour has been preordained — and what about my own four marriages as preordained by a simple game of needle and thread — what could I have done to change any of it?*

Ben and Mary had a medical practice to look after. Ben proceeded to teach Mary more than what is required of an assistant. He was trying to teach her what he knew as a doctor. He had an extensive library and pointed out books for her to read. He introduced her to the physician's medical library where she would go to do research about everything and anything, including research for her own midwifery knowledge and skills. There were medical journals coming in the mail and Mary took them home to become her bathroom library where she had daily reading sessions on the latest information about surgeries, psychotherapy, and much more. She went to school in evenings to take courses she thought she needed. Life was full. It was exciting with so much to learn. There was little time for grieving.

Patients needed care and Ben relied on Mary every day, twenty-four hours a day to help and to fill in for him when necessary. Then there were the births that Mary need to attend. Sometimes, she was awake for several days and when she arrived home, her back hit the mattress in pain. Mary was getting a lesson in birth, death and everything in between. Trying to be helpful with no judgment was a way of life.

Ben's ex-wife who was a lawyer, made storms regularly. She was making a career of how to disrupt his life. She made his life a living hell as much as possible. He had given her all the assets of the marriage and took all the debts when they divorced, but she wanted more and continued the harassment. His sons were growing up being told he was a cash cow for them to exploit. When they did not get all they wanted, they would not talk with him and they would blame Mary. Outside of his medical practice, his life was in turmoil, trying to appease his family. The stress took a toll on Ben. He had a failing heart that had become enlarged. He was daily in danger of losing his life, but his ex-wife's harassment continued. Mary asked Ben to discontinue his life insurance and tell his ex-wife just in case that's what she was after. He did so.

Early in the relationship, Ben took Mary and her youngest daughter to visit his mother and brother on the other side of the continent. They were met at the airport by Ben's brother and mother. The brother immediately gave Ben a dressing down for bringing Mary, right in front of Mary as though her feelings did not matter. His mother stood by silently with a look on her face that was embarrassment, but she did not extend a welcome to Mary. Ben was shocked. He had not expected this kind of greeting after being away for years.

Mary was still thinking Ben's mother was just embarrassed. She was not yet prepared to be so blatantly rejected by another mother.

Ben had been bragging to Mary about his brother's maple syrup farm that he farmed only with horses for help. They went there for overnight regardless that the brother had made it clear Mary was not a welcome guest. Mary and her daughter were told to sleep in a room upstairs. The mattresses on the floor were covered with old urine and the floor had mouse droppings everywhere.

The next day, they traveled to Ben's mother's county home. It was in a beautiful area of white and green homes sprinkled in the hills surrounded by plush green forests. Mary was grateful that the sleeping arrangement was clean.

Ben's mother on the surface was pleasant, so Mary figured it was safe to join Ben and his mother in a sitting room where they were in conversation. As she entered the doorway, the conversation stopped and the looks on both faces told Mary not to enter.

It was only later, back home that Ben revealed to Mary that his mother was convinced Mary, a woman with so many children, was simply after his money. He had no money but his potential for money was possible if his family did not take every penny. On the other hand, Ben's mother did have money and Ben would inherit a portion of it. Furthermore, she was unforgiving of her son for getting a divorce, regardless that her other two sons were divorced and remarried. Her reasoning was that she could not handle more divorces in her family — it had nothing to do with the fact that she thought Ben's ex-wife was sick and dangerous.

Ben admitted that his mother had elicited a promise from him that he would *never* marry Mary.

Never-the-less, when the mother visited Ben, Mary took care of taking her to medical appointments at Ben's request.

After one afternoon of spending hours taking the woman to see a doctor, Mary needed to pick up a prescription and deliver it to her in the evening. Ben's mother refused to look up, she read a newspaper and refused to acknowledge Mary or the delivery of her prescription. Mary had enough of being insulted. After that, Mary refused to visit the woman when she visited.

Over the years, Mary and Ben always lived in separate apartments. He was conflicted. He wanted a relationship with Mary but was bound by a promise to his mother and the toll of an ex-wife and children. He lived in turmoil of never being able to relax and do what might be good for himself.

They worked together for more than twenty years. Then Ben got sick. His heart was beyond repair. He was in congenital heart failure. His sons were now adults. After keeping Ben hostage, no family member would look after him when he was ill even though he asked them for help.

Ben was too ill to live by himself. As a doctor, he knew too much and did not want to be hospitalized for any reason, nor did he want an emergency team to come to his aid. Mary moved him into her home.

By then, Ben's mother had died and could not object. His brothers, sisters, children and ex-wife were all glad not to have to look after him. Suddenly, they were friendly to Mary. At the same time, no one visited him. Ben commented many times that after all the years of rejection, Mary was the only person willing to look after him.

For two years they enjoyed being in the same home. It was not perfect. He had bouts of almost dying and needed help just to live through the night. They enjoyed television —Mary fell asleep in every movie. He enjoyed baseball games. He never had his own television, so this was new to him. They cooked soups and other things together when he was feeling okay. It was a platonic relationship—he was too ill and she was not thinking of him as a possible lover anymore. Her only wish was to keep him alive and healthy.

There were no secrets anymore between them. Mary often accompanied Ben to the bathroom to assist him. Often that is when she would sit on a chair while he was on the toilet and they would have a joking time, laughing at themselves and everything else. One evening on the way to the bathroom, Ben turned around and said, "Get lost. I want to live."

He said to Mary, "An out of body person was behind me and told me I am going to die."

Mary had not heard it, but she believed.

He continued, "I told him to get lost, I want to live." He laughed. "I'm not dying yet."

Ben loved to go to the beach. Every nice day they would sit by the water and watch the tides and hear the swish of the waves on the sand. It felt like a healing time. They would walk the dog along the seawall. Ben walked, expecting to build his strength and recover from his illness. There were benches along the seawall where they would sit and talk, then continue just a little farther. He was full of hope in those days.

One autumn afternoon on the way to the beach, a voice in the back seat of the car said, *"You are going to die."*

The voice was as clear as if a real person was speaking from the back seat. There was no one there. This time, Mary heard it, too. Ben and Mary looked at each other and asked, "Did you hear that?" They both agreed that they heard it. Astounded, they were silent, not knowing what to say.

For two years she had cared for Ben. She always slept on the sofa in the same room. Then one night she woke up with a strange feeling. She walked over to him. He looked so small and shrunken in his bed. She took his thin hand in hers. He opened his eyes and smiled. Ben's eyes were innocent, pure, clear love. His whole face was at peace. Ben had transcended. He was still in his body but he was no longer mortal. He looked at Mary with unworldly, heavenly beautiful love. He smiled and said, *"I love you."*

She went back to her bed. He died in the morning while she slept.

For two years Mary lacked sleep. She had woken up every two hours to check up on Ben. The morning he died, she slept in an abnormally deep sleep for six hours while he died.

She washed away one tear that had dried on his cheek.

The next sleep she had, she woke up to having him clearly laying beside her. Since she was sleeping on the sofa, he was laying beside her by floating in the air with nothing solid below him. As she was looking at him, he was absolutely clear in full color, then he slowly faded until he disappeared. When he died, his white wavy hair was long to his shoulders, which was two years growth, but in astral form he had short hair like he wore it for many years as a young man.

Then the fun began:

Ben preferred radio rather than television. Mary's television lost its pictures and became a radio for a week.

Mary and her sister were discussing putting the urn with the ashes of Mary's beloved Miniature Schnauzer in the coffin with Ben at the time of burial. They heard a loud crash in the kitchen. On investigation, they discovered the wooden Miniature Schnauzer with a very

strong magnetic backing that had been on the refrigerator door and was so strong that Mary had never been able to move it, was now laying on the floor.

Coins were piling up after being found everywhere inside and outside. Mary had vacuumed under the upholstered chair that Ben sat in a lot. After the vacuuming, she found coins under the chair when no one had sat in the chair. With the many coins found, Mary filled the wishing well in a large sculpture that he had admired.

Messages started. The first message was to tell Mary that he had kept her asleep on purpose while he died.

By automatic writing, Mary wrote down the information the deceased Ben wanted to let everyone know about the death experience. He especially wanted everyone to know **HE IS VERY MUCH ALIVE.**

It was declared a common-law marriage legally because of the years shared and two years actually living together under the same roof. Mary wondered if marriage by default could really be her fourth marriage as predicted by a needle and thread.

It kind of did not matter because in sharing more than twenty years, she had known a man who was love.

chapter eleven

Secrets

It was a quiet evening in the hospital ward where Mary was now working. The patients were bedded down for the night and seemed comfortable. There were no new patients expected for the next while. Mary was on her break, but instead of going to the lounge for a coffee or to rest, she decided to use her personal computer for a look at her family photos. She scanned through a few of her grandchildren and then wandered through some older photos.

A patient's bell rang. A patient was needing something. She sprang up to go and take care of the patient regardless that she was on a break because no other personnel was available.

When she got back to her station at the desk, she realized she had left her computer open. She was stunned as she stared at the picture on the screen and wondered — *How did my picture get up there?* She stood over the computer with the question shouting at her. Slowly, she realized the picture was of her grandmother, her mother's mother, the same woman she had wondered all her life if she was her. The picture was not of Mary.

Mary felt a bit shaken as she realized she had briefly been in an altered state of mind when she looked at her grandmother's picture. She continued to stare at the picture that now she saw as her grandmother's picture. The old question arose — *Why? Why had I approached my computer and thought the picture was of me? Am I really my own grandmother? — a woman who lost her children at such a young age? Was this the answer, finally? I don't want to think about it.*

She remembered that years ago her grandfather had appeared in a lucid dream to answer her question. He simply said to Mary, *"Get on with your life."* She had gladly done so.

"What's your secret?'

In the middle of putting together a spaghetti sauce, the telephone rang. Mary's sister's cheerful voice burst through the line in excitement with that absurd question.

Stunned, Mary's mind raced, wondering — *how did she guess? Was it intuition?*

"I have no secret. My life's an open book." Mary responded.

That was a giant lie because she never shared her private life with anyone and would not start now.

Just a few minutes before her sister called, Mary had come in from a walk on the beach with her dog and heard her cousin's cheerful voice across the room, leaving a message on her answering machine. "Just checking on how you are doing. I'll call later."

Feeling bare and intruded upon, Mary wondered how two relatives were picking up on her distress and strong desire to run away, but not knowing where to go. She just wanted to be left alone. Her secret was never going to be shared or discussed. The secret would forever be a secret.

Her sister was rattling on cheerfully, "My dog woke me up and I don't know the end of my dream. You might have the answer. You came for a visit with one bag. You did not want to be in a bedroom. I did not know if you were coming or going. You just wanted to talk, so we went into the garden. You said you had met a person and wondered how the family would feel about the relationship. And then my dog woke me up."

"Man or woman?" Mary laughed.

"Woman with a man's body."

"And what does the person look like?"

"Nice looking. Dressed like a woman. Neat. Sort of young."

"I don't have any interest in a relationship with a cross gender person."

"They are not to be afraid of."

"Of course not, but that's not what I mean. I just prefer heterosexual relationships. What was your advice?"

"I told you that you could have the benefit of a woman friend and a sexual relationship with the man."

Mary burst into loud laughter. "It sounds too absurd."

Her sister continued, "But I want to know the rest of the story in my dream."

"I've got no secret. So I can't help you."

"Maybe you can use it in your writing and give it an ending.

"I don't think I'll include your dream. I already have my new story outlined. It's a novel this time. Maybe you are picking up that I want to run away from this house because they cut down the tree in front of my door. I tried to save it but they would not listen to my reasoning."

"They own the house. They can cut down a tree."

"I know they own the house and can cut down a tree. But, that tree wasn't harming anyone. It had rights to live."

"They own the house."

"I know, but I am really angry anyway that they would cut down a healthy mountain ash tree. It was a beautiful tree. Birds love the red berries. I would watch the many types of birds that came to the tree and it provided the only shade I have on the patio in the heat of summer. Now I look out onto hydro and telephone wires and a telephone pole instead of the tree. They won't negotiate about the life of a tree even though its roots were holding up a corner of the steep hill the house is on. I thought it was saving that corner from erosion in our torrential rains."

With the conversation successfully turned to her tree, Mary was relieved that a secret was no longer the topic.

On the beach in the evening, Mary walked with her dog on the sand by the incoming waves. She was experiencing overwhelming and tearful emotions drowned out by the sound of splashing water. Interpreting her sister's dream, it seemed to be too invasive. Her secret was that she had fantasized about a certain man by day and dreamed about him at night for years. Over time, she hoped it would at least turn into a lifetime of intimate friendship—the woman and man in her sister's dream rolled into one. More than that, Mary had wondered how to explain the relationship with a younger man to her family if it ever happened as a long relationship.

It was disturbing that in a dream, her sister was somehow penetrating a privacy across more than a thousand physical miles, only to be stopped by a dog. Mary was grateful to the dog. She was determined that her business was nobody's business.

What was the latest on her secret? One afternoon her secret lover just happened to be crossing her path when they stopped to talk. Then he asked if she would accept a hug before parting. She hesitated because normally she was not the type of person to go around hugging people.

She relented. "Okay."

His arms wrapped around her and she responded stiffly at first. As the hug continued longer than expected, she melted into his chest as though drawn by a magnet. For the first time in her life she felt at home—totally and completely at home. His strong arms tightened, drawing her even closer. She responded by relaxing all her being into his chest and felt him kiss the top of her head. He whispered into her hair. What he was saying, she could not hear. Then he released her and they went their separate ways as though nothing important had happened.

During the night, Mary was awakened suddenly out of a sound sleep with a strong feeling of being hugged. The hug was more than just a hug—it was deeper than just a physical union. He had penetrated her soul with a hug. She was now attached to him in a union of love at the deepest place possible.

She was awake now and spent the next hours wondering — *why and how was the attachment to him so strong and so complete? Have we known each other in another lifetime? Were we lovers or man and wife in another lifetime? Why now? Why so late in this life? Why have we not met in our younger years and married and had a family together? What is this all about? Why did I have to go through all those troublesome relationships? Why did I have to be lonely all my life in relationships of the past? Why am I suddenly in love — really in love for the first time in my life? And what about him? Is he feeling any of the same feelings? Is he wondering, too?*

The only thing she knew was that his hug was like nothing she had ever known before. She had never been hugged like he had hugged her. She had never felt the attachment to another person that she now felt all because of the feeling of his arms surrounding her and the feeling of being completely at home on his chest. It was stronger now in the night. Her soul found love. It was no longer a fantasy. She was surrendering into soul love.

It was many months until meeting again. During that time, Mary decided it had all been a mistake and tried hard to forget him and his hug. One evening just when she thought she was being successful, he telephoned. She hesitated again. This time she told him she was afraid of getting hurt. She was genuinely scared of reopening all the feelings for him. The feelings had not really gone away, they had merely been submerged, so after pausing and breathing heavily with indecision over several minutes, she agreed to meet him.

In their meetings over the next few weeks, he would be a man of many firsts. He held her hand while she got out of the car. He held her hand to help her into a car. No man had ever held her hand before to help her in any situation and especially never to get in or out of a vehicle.

He asked her what she was thinking? No other man had ever asked her or cared about her thoughts.

He said she was a sweetheart. She had never been called a name of endearment before.

He was a complete gentleman and at the same time he had strength in every movement which was a combination that was new and so sexy. She had never before known this kind of man.

He was taking care of all the craved tenderness and sense of caring that she had never known before him.

She was truly in love for the first time in her life. Just the sight of him made her heart jump because she saw him as the handsomest man on earth. Each time she saw him, he got more and more handsome.

She had five books about sex in her book collection but had never felt the need to study them while in any former relationship. Now, she pulled the books down and read every page, trying to understand what to do to be the best lover. She wanted to really understand the anatomy of a man and how to satisfy him, to give to him and not just take.

After hours of reading and studying pictures of anatomy and positions of sex, she decided that every man must have personal likes and dislikes, so she would ask him to teach her what he needs. She looked forward with excitement and anticipation of greater sex exploration than he and she had ever known. She waited.

There were weeks of silence. During that time, a foreboding was slowly overshadowing anticipation of the opportunity to please him. It seemed ironic that she had gotten herself ready for the best sex ever, and it was not going to happen. Once again, her life was lonely — seemingly more acute now.

Then they met by accident on the street.

"We have to talk," he said.

"Is it bad news?" she asked.

He did not look at her but turned his gaze to the sky. "No … just a talk."

A few moments of silence and he did look at her. His face was drained of light. His eyes were dull with sadness. "It was a mistake."

She was stunned and waited for what was to follow.

He continued, "You and me. It was a mistake."

She was silent — what could she say when confronted with such a conclusion?

"I'll call you," he said.

He did not call. It was over and she would never know why. She could only wonder how and why? The last time they were together, he had taken her into his arms and given her a special hug just before they parted. She had melted into his chest just like the first time he hugged her. Indelible in her memory was his face that had been relaxed and smiling as though he was happy.

It had started with a hug and ended with a hug. He left no trace except for what lingered in her heart. All the years of hoping for long, warm summer evenings together under the stars just talking — walks in the woods and laying a blanket on the ground somewhere — and waking up to his touch—and to be able to reach over and caress his hair—imagining sex happening at any time, any place—all gone.

Weeks later, he called to say, "We need to talk."

They met. He explained, "I don't want to hurt you, but I think you love me more than I love you. I don't love you. If you can accept that I am always free, I can fill more of your fantasies."

She asked, "Have you ever loved?"

"In my young years. I choose not to in my older years."

"I don't expect you to marry me."

"You mean companionship is enough?"

Mary nodded.

There was a few moments of silence. Then she said, "I made a mistake. You have been simply a figment of my fantasy. Today and tomorrow, all that matters is love. I am finished with drama."

Mary decided to wear her Carnelian ring that she had put away years ago. She looked for it and found the Carnelian stone had been removed—it was gone. The ring lay in two pieces—broken in half.

Just when Mary thought she was through with drama, her daughter stood in front of her. Her eyes were tortured. Her face looked drained. She trembled with distress. "How could you? All those men! You made my life miserable with all those changes, changing our name, moving around, and all those men. How could you? And all that spirit stuff. I have my two feet on the ground. All I want to do is work and take care of my family. I don't believe in your stuff."

Mary stood silently. This was not new news. Sympathy for her daughter and what she had not been able to give her had always bothered her. She had tried. This was the daughter who got smacked and knocked into a bathtub by husband three because she defended her sister. Mary waited for the tirade to end. When it did, she watched her daughter walk away, having emptied herself of her childhood hurts.

Mary wondered how could she explain to her daughter who had managed to have one stable, loving marriage and children in one marriage. Times were different. There was no social media—no computers—not even telephones in many homes. Attitudes about marriage, divorce, sex and single parenthood changed entirely since her children grew up. There was no way to really explain what it was like to be a single parent—how women of divorce or having gotten pregnant outside of marriage were thought to be whores and treated like they were unfit as human beings. There was no convincing anyone about experiences with spirits or anything else, but she was surprised that her own daughter thought she was nuts, living in a wayward reality. There was no way to explain and have someone else understand unless they walked in her footsteps. She could not change a thing at the end of it all. She had no answer.

Mary thought about her life as she walked on the sand and listened to the ocean swishing onto the shore. Having given up a lifelong fantasy of having love, she cried, washing it all away. She thought about how she had children and grandchildren, but never a stable home. She was the only constant in her children's lives. She could offer her children no father to balance their home life. Along the way, she had always given everything material away and kept nothing for herself. She relied on a spiritual power to keep everyone safe. Mary thought about how in her work, she had seen facets of life from birth to death. She wondered why, in this cosmos made of love, that genuine, unconditional love between man and woman is so hard to come by.

spirit speaks:
I am still here, watching over her. What is a dream? What is fantasy? What is truth? What is an illusion? Like fluffy balls of dandelion seeds that ripen and blow off in the wind; they float for a while and then fly away. Where they land is the start of golden, sunny new life.

The last domino was played. Every spring, she will walk among the golden, wild dandelions that spring up out of the mud and dust with renewed strength to live and multiply, reminding her there is always a new day. Everywhere she goes, she plants roses. She is a rose — softly sensitive within, with outward resilience of a daisy.

Books published by Daisy Harriette Heisler, also published
as H.T.A. Heisler and Daisy H.T.A. Heisler

doctor ken
*a true story about a man
and the Hippocratic Oath
— story told by H.T.A. Heisler
— with writings by Kehnroth Schramm, M.D.*

Packets of Seeds
*Messages from Kehnroth Schramm, M.D.
describing Life after Passing
(compiled and edited by H.T.A. Heisler)*

Awakening Memories
Short Stories

The Innkeeper's Daughter
*a Christmas Story and Music Score
fictional story about the girl who was present
at the birth of Jesus and is the foundation for the
included musical score
watercolour illustrations throughout the book
(intended for children or adults playing an instrument or for voice
— not intended as a picture book for young children)*

Rescue Millie
*and The Science of Dogs
a true story about rescuing a homeless dog*
co-author: Taylor J. Sims
co-author: Kayden K. Montaine

website: www.DaisyHarrietteHeisler.com